MED CENTER

D1308061

MED CENTER

MED CENTER

DIANE HOH

poison

SCHOLASTIC INC.
New York Toronto London Auckland Sydney

ISBN 0-590-89755-1

12 11 10 9 8 7 6 5 4 3 2 1   7 8 9/9 0 1 2/0

Printed in the U.S.A.

First Scholastic printing, March 1997

prologue

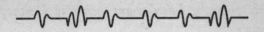

I have to be careful. And patient. One at a time, that's the only way. More than one missing might arouse suspicion. This way, they're all clueless.

It's hard to go so slowly.

Someone always seems to be watching. But people only see what they want to see. Someone could be looking straight at me when I slip one into my pocket, but they wouldn't think anything of it. Most people are too busy thinking about themselves to really pay attention to details.

I didn't measure any of it. Why would I? A little in this one, a little more in that one, a lot more in another . . . variety is the spice of life, after all. I was careful, at first. I don't want people dropping like flies. That would make it too easy for them. I want them confused. That's how I felt when all my dreams suddenly turned to ashes.

It would have been more fun to do everything all at once. Lining all of them up in a row on my kitchen table, like soldiers going off to war. Which, of course, they are. Off to my war.

But that would have been foolish. One at a time, that's the only way.

My humiliation was public. Everyone knew. Everyone gossiped about it. This will teach them not to whisper behind my back, not to look at me with sympathy. I don't want their pity. I want justice.

If Med Center is ruined by scandal, the people who work there will suffer, too. All of the people who work there. And that's what I want.

chapter
1

—〰〰〰〰〰—

The final track meet of the season was held in Grant, Massachusetts, on Memorial Day weekend. Although it was a high school event, it was held in the stadium at Grant University which had more seating space.

Fans were out in force for the meet. On a blue-skied Saturday afternoon, the stadium was packed with students, teachers, and supporters. Although the band never played at track meets, the cheerleaders were there. Abby O'Connor, in a white pleated skirt and blue-and-white tank top, had just completed a series of cartwheels in front of the crowd.

As she stood upright, her dark, curly hair tousled, her eyes bright with excitement, Abby searched the stands for her best friend, Susannah Grant. Susannah attended a private day school instead of Grant High, but she had promised to attend today's meet.

Abby found her almost immediately. Although Susannah wasn't aware of it, she was the sort of person you noticed in a crowd. Tall, slender, her fair, wavy hair hanging loose around her lovely, oval face, she was sitting near the middle of the bleachers between her twin brother, Samuel Grant III, and Kate Thompson, a friend and fellow volunteer at Med Center.

It wasn't the expensive, tailored white shorts and red crop top she was wearing that called attention to Susannah. And it wasn't the golden tan or the incredibly bright blue eyes. It was, Abby thought, the way she carried herself — the way her mother had taught her — with her head high but a smile on her face. Still, while that look drew attention to Susannah, Abby knew that most people seldom took the time to get to know her well. They were intimidated by the Grant name.

Abby's eyes moved to Sid, parked in his wheelchair in the aisle next to Sam. Sweet, gorgeous Sid. Abby's smile widened as she waved to him and he waved back. They were attending a party that evening at Jeremy Barlow's house, even if Grant didn't win the meet.

But they *would* win. They had the best relay team in the state. They hadn't lost once this year and wouldn't lose today, either, because there was Will Jackson, in his blue-and-white track uniform. He was bouncing around on his toes, warming up. While everyone on the team was fast, it was tall, lanky Will who was the linchpin, and everyone knew it.

Abby glanced up into the stands again to see if Susannah was watching Will. Of course she was. Any time Will was in the vicinity, Susannah's eyes were drawn to him like a magnet. Will had stopped bouncing around. He was rubbing his temples, as if he had a headache. Maybe because he was facing into the sun.

Abby hoped that was all it was. If Will wasn't feeling well, they *could* lose this meet. The party at Jeremy's wouldn't be as much fun if they lost. Jeremy's parties weren't always a guaranteed blast, anyway. He wasn't exactly the host with the most. He was only having this party tonight because his father had gone out of town. Thomas Barlow, a world-renowned cardiologist, was giving a speech at a medical convention in California. "Might as well take advantage of an empty house," Jeremy had told Abby, Susannah, and Kate.

They needed a win this afternoon to keep the party spirit going tonight, especially if Jeremy was in a bad mood.

Will was still rubbing his temples. Abby, standing nearby on the sidelines, thought he looked a little disoriented. That's ridiculous, she decided, then took two steps backward to join the other cheerleaders in a rousing cheer for each of the four members of the relay team.

Up in the bleachers, Susannah Grant frowned, raised a hand to shield her eyes against the sun, and said to her tall, blond brother, "Something's wrong with Will."

"With Will?" Sam's eyes were exactly the same shade of blue as his sister's, but his hair had been bleached almost white by the sun. He spent a lot more time outside golfing, swimming, playing tennis, than Susannah. "He looks okay to me."

"I think she's right," Kate Thompson said from beside Susannah. Removing her sunglasses, she studied Will. "He looks shaky. And why is he rubbing his temples?"

"Sun's in his eyes," Sid said from the aisle. "He'll be okay once he gets going. He'd better be."

From behind them, Jeremy said flatly, "If they lose, it'll ruin my party."

"They're not going to lose," Sam laughed. "When has this relay team ever lost? It makes me wish I went to Grant High instead of private school. It'd be a blast to be part of Will's team."

"Assuming you were fast enough," Sid said dryly.

"I'm fast enough." Sam's voice bore the confidence of an assured athlete.

"I'll just bet you are." Like Susannah, Kate Thompson was tall and slender. Unlike Susannah, she was dressed in inexpensive denim cut-offs and a white T-shirt. But even in such ordinary clothing, Kate Thompson had style. She had a beautiful face, with high, well-sculpted cheekbones and smooth, clear skin. Her dark, shoulder-length hair, often cornrowed, was loose on this warm afternoon, worn in a smooth, thick, angled cut. Her skin, like Will's, was dark, as were her eyes. "Everyone knows Samuel Grant III has been chased by more females than any guy in town. You *must* be fast or else you'd have been caught by now."

Susannah laughed. "He's been caught more than once. He always slips away, though. Kind of like an eel. I thought Lily Dolan was keeping him in her net, but I don't see her around here anywhere."

"She's working. At Emsee," Sam told them. Emsee was a popular nickname for Med Center, the huge medical complex where Susannah and Abby, along with Kate, volunteered. Will was one of the paramedics, the youngest on any of the teams. "But she might make it to the party later. She said she'd try."

Lily Dolan, a stunning, popular, nurse's aide at the medical complex, had recently, with the help of a social worker friend of Abby's, moved out of her abusive father's home and into a garage apartment at Abby's house.

Susannah glanced at Sam in an attempt to read the expression on his face. He had fallen hard for Lily, a surprise to everyone. Especially, she thought, Sam himself. He added, "She's trying to save enough money to attend Grant U, and works a lot of overtime. She keeps telling me I shouldn't sit around the house waiting for her, that I should just do my own thing."

"Well, you should," Kate said. "Lily means it. She knows fun is your thing, and she doesn't have time for it. I know the feeling." She, like Lily, had plans. If becoming a doctor someday meant working harder in the meantime than most people, studying harder than most people, well, fine. Nothing was going to keep Kate Thompson from having what she wanted. She knew Lily felt the same way.

"So you might be going to Jeremy's party alone?" Susannah asked Sam.

"Looks that way," Sam said gloomily.

Susannah smiled. If Sam walked into that party alone, Callie Matthews would be lying in wait for him. Without Lily's protective presence, Callie would pursue Sam mercilessly. Not that Sam couldn't handle it. He'd had plenty of experience with girls. Far more than his twin had had with guys.

"So, you decided not to run today, Costello?" a boy said lightly as he passed Sid's wheelchair.

Without missing a beat, Sid answered just as lightly, "Couldn't find my other track shoe." The boy laughed and clapped him on the shoulder.

Sam watched the exchange with admiration. A former athlete at Grant High, Sid Costello hadn't had the use of his legs since he'd fallen from the water tower the previous summer. He'd gone through a difficult time, and to hear him joking about his misfortune with a friend was startling to Sam. If he, also an athlete, ever found himself in a wheelchair, he thought he would probably lose his mind.

Sid almost had, at first. But then he'd met Abby O'Connor, at Rehab, where he'd been a patient and where Abby did most of her volunteering. The attraction had been immediate. Abby's bubbly personality had slowly pulled Sid out of the black hole he was in. His attitude had changed. So much so, that now his friends knew it was safe to kid him about his situation. As astonishing as Sam found that, it was a big relief. He spent a lot of time with Sid, hauling him and his wheelchair around town. It made it easier knowing Sid's sense of humor was still intact.

Sid had recently been discharged from Rehab and was living at home again, but he returned to the complex six days a week for physical therapy.

Though he'd never said so, Sam really admired Sid. And O'Connor, too. Abby was responsible for a lot of the progress Sid had made.

"They're starting!" Kate cried.

Sam turned his attention to the track.

The race was closer than expected. After three tense laps, the two runners from the opposing teams were neck and neck when Will, the last to run, was handed the baton. He flew out onto the track as if he'd been shot from a cannon, his legs churning, arms pumping, eyes straight ahead. His opponent was right behind him.

The stadium rang with shrieks and shouts in support of Will. The cheerleaders jumped up and down, clapping their hands and urging him on.

On he flew, as if his track shoes had wings.

"Attaboy, Will!" Sam shouted. "That finish line belongs to you now. Go for it!"

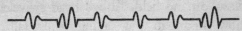

Susannah hadn't taken her eyes off Will for an instant. But she still couldn't have described afterwards exactly how it happened. She was too shocked to take it all in clearly.

One minute, Will was flying along the track. The next minute, he was staggering, his momentum gone. His right hand, holding the baton, went to his right temple. The other hand clutched his stomach.

Then he collapsed.

Susannah cried out. Her hands flew to her mouth.

Following shouts of surprise and dismay from the crowd, a heavy blanket of anxious silence descended upon the stadium.

The opposing runner kept going, sweeping on to the finish line while coaches and teammates rushed to Will's side.

"I've got to go down there," Susannah said, and tried to push past Sam.

He resisted her push. "You'll just be in the way. You're a volunteer at the hospital, Susannah, not a doctor. Let the professionals handle Will. It's probably just the heat."

"It's not that hot," she argued, but she stayed where she was. Sam was probably right. She'd be in the way.

Below, on the field, Abby's head swiveled to see how Susannah was taking Will's fall. She wanted to run up and comfort her best friend, but she quickly decided the best thing she could do for Susannah now was stay and see how Will was. Abby sighed. Susannah and Will's relationship was so different from hers with Sid. She and Sid were very open about their feelings. And for the most part, people were supportive. But while Abby and Sid's relationship, except for a few glitches, was progressing smoothly, Susannah and Will's never had. Sometimes, like lately, they got along fine. Other times, they let the tiniest little things get to them, guarding against feelings neither was sure they wanted to have.

There were good reasons for their caution, Abby knew that. There was the money thing, of course. Susannah lived in a mansion, with lush gardens, a household staff, an Olympic-sized swimming pool, and a tennis court. It even had a name, Linden Hall, and sat high on a hill overlooking the city.

Will, however, lived in a small, white house in Eastridge, a community on the east side of the city where most of the African-Americans in Grant lived.

As attracted as Susannah and Will were to each other, and as much as they had in common, both of them attractive and smart and compassionate, neither seemed fully convinced yet that giving in to their feelings was a smart move.

There were those times, Abby knew, when Susannah was ready to throw caution to the wind and show the whole world how she felt about Will Jackson. But those always seemed to be the moments when Will wasn't ready. He held back, and Abby sensed that it was because he was afraid of making life in Grant uncomfortable for Susannah.

Watching Will now, Abby thought — not for the first time — Sid and I are lucky. Stupid people like Callie Matthews might ask dumb questions because of his wheelchair, but that's just curiosity, not the disapproval that Susannah and Will might face.

Up in the bleachers, Susannah wondered what could be wrong with Will. It was very obvious that he hadn't tripped. He'd collapsed, for no apparent reason. Was he sick?

"That's why he was rubbing his temples," Kate said suddenly. "There was something wrong even before he came out on the track. He shouldn't have tried running."

"He knew this was an important meet," Susannah said, her eyes never once leaving the scene on the track. "He was excited about this race, and although he kept saying relay is a team effort, he had to know they'd never win without him."

And they hadn't. Will's opponent had already reached the finish line. Grant had lost.

From his seat in the aisle, Sid said, "He's not getting up. They're putting him on a stretcher. Must be taking him to Med Center."

"Then he really *is* sick," Susannah murmured. More emphatically, she said, "*I'm* going with them. Kate, are you coming?"

"Yep."

This time, Sam didn't argue with Susannah. Instead, he decided to go, too, offering to drive Sid and Jeremy to the complex.

Abby was waiting for Susannah and Kate at the foot of the bleachers. "No one knows what's wrong with him," she said hastily, seeing the stricken look on Susannah's face. "Everyone seems to think it's the heat."

"It's *not* that hot," Susannah repeated testily. "It has to be something else."

Susannah and Kate, the only two high school volunteers who had completed the necessary classes and tests required for admittance into trauma and treatment rooms, were standing just inside the door of Will's white-walled cubicle at

Med Center. Astrid Thompson, Kate's mother and E.R.'s head nurse, was also in the room. Two other nurses, Patsy Keene and Roberta Swickert, were assisting the doctor.

Will, fully conscious but complaining of stomach pain, had been rushed to Grant Memorial, the largest of the hospitals in the huge Medical Center complex of eighteen buildings, and the only one with a fully equipped Emergency Center. There, he had been moved from the stretcher to one of the examination tables. Dr. Izbecki had checked him over carefully, ordered the blood tests necessary for a preliminary diagnosis in any emergency case, and administered an electrocardiogram to rule out a heart problem. Astrid had asked what Will had eaten and drunk before the race, if he'd had enough sleep the night before, if he'd been feeling ill recently. None of Will's answers provided any clue about what had struck him down.

Now Will lay quietly, awaiting the results of his tests and hopefully, a diagnosis.

The tests took a while. On a holiday weekend with near-drownings, car accidents, and heatstroke, the lab was overtaxed.

When they did arrive, the test results showed nothing. There seemed to be no apparent physiological reason for Will's collapse.

Dr. Izbecki announced that it had to be something Will had eaten.

"Something he ate?" Susannah echoed. "What could he have eaten that would make him this sick?"

"I'm not sick," Will protested weakly from where he lay on the table. "I don't *get* sick. I must have tripped. Gravel or something . . ." His voice faded away.

"That wouldn't explain your stomach cramps," Dr. Izbecki pointed out. "Or the headache you said you had earlier."

Will wasn't ready to give in. "The headache was from last night. I stayed up too late, studying for finals. And as for my stomach, maybe I hit it on something when I fell."

"You were sick *before* you fell," Kate chimed in. "Anyone could see that. Quit arguing with the doctor and do what he tells you to do."

"I'm going to give you something to soothe those cramps," Dr. Izbecki said as Nurse Keene removed the blood pressure cuff from Will's upper arm. "And something for the headache you complained about. You can pick up the medications at the desk on the way out. I'd take it easy the rest of the day. No more races."

"Never mind the headache stuff. We've got plenty at home. As for my stomach, are you talking about the pink stuff that tastes like chalk?"

Izbecki grinned. "That's the stuff. Take it, Will. And go home. Go to bed." He hurried off to another patient.

Will groaned again, but not from pain this time. "I blew it! I could practically smell the finish line, and I blew it."

"It wasn't your fault," Susannah said, moving forward to take one of his hands in hers. "You were sick."

"I'm *not* sick!"

Susannah grinned. Will seemed much better now. He was okay. Something he ate . . . that's all it was.

"So, what *did* you eat this morning?" she asked when she, Kate, and Abby were walking Will to the parking garage. Kate, like Will, lived in Eastridge, and had offered to drive Will and his truck home. Abby had been waiting outside the cubicle. As soon as Sam, Jeremy, and Sid learned that Will would be okay, they'd left for Jeremy's house to begin party preparations.

Will shrugged in response to Susannah's question. He kept one hand on his stomach in a comforting gesture, but his walk was steady. He shifted the package of medication he was carrying into the crook of his elbow in order to hold Susannah's hand and said, "I didn't eat *enough*. I think that's the problem. I usually stoke up before a race, with pasta, whatever. But I had a rotten headache this morning and didn't feel like eating. All I could handle was coffee and a bagel. Big mistake. The pain in my gut was probably from an empty stomach."

"Maybe the bagel was bad," Kate suggested. "Moldy, or something?"

Will sent her a look of disgust. "Like I'd eat something that was moldy. You think I just dump food into my mouth without checking it out first?"

Kate laughed. "Get real. You are a seventeen-year-old male. A veritable mass of hormones and appetites. So yes, I think food goes into your mouth around the clock as if it were on a conveyor belt, and no, I do not think you check out every morsel before you vacuum it up."

Will laughed then, too. "You're right. Maybe the bagel was a little past its prime. From now on, I *will* check."

"Sure you will." They had reached Will's truck in the staff parking lot. Kate held the passenger's door open for him. "And I'm gonna be appointed Chief of Staff at this hospital tomorrow."

"Congratulations," Will said, and climbed into the truck.

Susannah lingered by the door for a few minutes while Kate went around to the driver's side. Will rolled his window down and extended his hand to entwine Susannah's fingers in his. "Looks like I won't be seeing you tonight," he said, regret in his voice. "Sorry about that. I feel better than I did, but . . ."

She nodded quickly. "It's okay. You don't want

18

to have a relapse. Eat something when you get home, okay? Chicken soup, maybe. And call me later. Abby and I will be on duty until six. You can call me when you feel better."

Kate started the truck with a roar.

"So," Will said awkwardly, "you're still going to go, right? To the party, I mean?"

Susannah hesitated. She didn't really feel like going, now that Will wasn't going to be there. But Jeremy was so sensitive. And that big, beautiful house had to feel *so* empty with his father out of town. She knew what *that* felt like.

"Yeah," she said reluctantly, "I think I'd better. For Jeremy."

He nodded. "You call me, then. When you get home. I'll be up."

"I will, I promise. I'm glad you're okay," Susannah said, and stood back to let the truck pull away.

"I can't go on duty like this," Abby said guiltily. She glanced down at her cheerleading uniform. "I forgot to bring clothes to change into. Can you drive me home first?"

Susannah rolled her eyes toward the sky. "Abby! You forgot your smock? Yesterday it was your ID. We're already late, and this is a holiday weekend. E.R.'s going to be really crazy. Astrid needs us."

"I remembered my badge." Abby fished in her shoulderbag and held up the plastic badge with her picture on it. "See? Better than nothing, right? C'mon, Susannah, in your car, the trip will only take ten minutes. Anyway, I want to see how my dad's doing."

Driving along Linden Hill Boulevard in the silver Mercedes-Benz convertible, with Abby chattering about the track meet, the party that night, and the Memorial Day picnic being held at Linden Hall the following day, Susannah fought to erase from her mind the image of Will collapsing on the track.

Will was *okay*. That was the important thing. He'd almost certainly be at the picnic tomorrow. It had been something he'd eaten. Dr. Izbecki had said so. So why was she torturing herself?

Because, she told herself, it scared me to death and I'm still not over it. Taking a deep breath and letting it out, Susannah forced herself to relax against the back of the seat and asked Abby, "So, what did you decide to wear tonight, the green or the blue?"

chapter
3

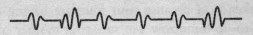

In the E.R. things were not as hectic as Susannah had feared.

"It's early yet," Astrid said as Susannah and Abby donned their pink smocks and signed in. "Last night wasn't too bad, either. But most of those celebrations were private parties. Tonight, we've got the public band concert and fireworks display on the riverbanks. Most of the city will be there. We'll have the usual drunk drivers, and we've already had two near-drownings — a fisherman and a nine-year-old. A few boat accidents on the river wouldn't surprise me, either." The tall, attractive head nurse shrugged and stuck a pencil behind one ear. "Well, I don't need to tell you. A warm weekend to kick off summer, and a holiday to boot . . . this place will be jumping. I wish you girls were going to be on tonight. That's when they're really going to need the extra help. I'm off at three, but so many other people took the weekend off, we might be a little understaffed. I told Schwinn to call me if things got too crazy, and I'd come in."

"I could stay," Susannah offered. If Will wasn't going to be at Jeremy's party, she might as well work.

Astrid shook her head. "Nope. You worked the last three weekends. I promised you this weekend off because your folks are having that big to-do tomorrow. I'm sure your mother could use your help getting ready. Half the town is going to be there."

Susannah hid a smile. Like her mother was going to prepare the picnic herself. The party-planner would do that, and the household staff would help. Caroline Grant would, of course, run things from behind the scenes. She would do it effectively, firmly but gently. "An iron fist in a velvet glove," Mary Margaret, one of the maids, called Caroline's way of asserting authority. But she said it with great affection. All of the staff was loyal to the Grant family.

The picnic would go smoothly, Susannah was sure of that. And not a single hair on her mother's head would slip out of place throughout the entire day, even if the wind blew. If the wind *dared* to blow on a picnic at Linden Hall.

"Well, I'm not offering to stay after my shift," Abby said cheerfully, "because I don't want to miss seeing Sid at Jeremy's party. Sorry, Astrid. I guess that makes me a selfish witch."

"That makes you normal," Astrid said, giving

Abby an affectionate smile. "So, are you off to Rehab now? Or are we lucky enough to have you with us today?"

"I'm staying here. A lot of patients at Rehab split. Weekend passes. It's pretty empty over there, so I'm yours. Where do you want me?"

"The two treatment rooms at the end of the hall could use straightening up. I had a couple of migraine patients in there, within minutes of each other. They both vomited. Sorry." Astrid's grin reminded Susannah of the sly smile Kate often displayed. Like mother, like daughter. "But you're just a lowly volunteer, Abby, and that's the kind of thing you people get stuck with."

Abby sighed. "I know, I know. So, where's my bucket and sponge?"

When she had trudged away, cleaning equipment in hand, Astrid sent Susannah to the waiting room to begin preliminary charts on people who were awaiting treatment.

Most of the complaints were typical weekend injuries or illnesses. There was a man with a broken arm. He had been trying to hang an American flag on his front porch and had fallen from a ladder. There were two young girls who had collided while skateboarding. They were not wearing protective headgear. Both had concussions and were being admitted for observation. There was a woman who had sprained her ankle removing laundry from a hillside clothesline, and an elderly man complaining of "heart palpitations."

The last patient, slumped in one of the blue plastic chairs, was a girl of about fifteen or sixteen. She had very short, spiked red hair, and a face as pale as her white T-shirt and shorts. She was holding both hands against her stomach in the same way that Will had been holding his just before he collapsed.

"What's the problem?" Susannah asked when she had written down the girl's name, address, and insurance information. "You don't look so hot. Are you here alone?"

The girl, whose name was Julie Whittier, shook her head. "I don't feel so great. My stomach hurts so bad, all I want to do is sleep. And that stinks, because I had big plans for this weekend."

"Got any idea why you're hurting?" Susannah was supposed to make notes on the admission form, and so far, Julie Whittier hadn't given her any solid information.

"I thought it was allergies, because it started when the weather warmed up and all that pollen was floating around. I have a reaction every spring. But, man, I never felt like *this* before!" She lifted her head with great effort to ask Susannah, "Can you give me something?"

"I'm just a volunteer. But one of the doctors

will take care of you as soon as there's a room free. Did you say you were here alone?"

The girl clutched at her stomach again. "Yeah, I'm on my own. I tried calling my parents. They both work at G.P." Grant Pharmaceuticals, one of the Grant family's companies. "But they were out of their offices. The pain got so bad, I couldn't wait. So I came here."

Telling the girl it shouldn't be too long, Susannah returned to the nurses' station to hand Nurse Roberta Swickert the information charts. "It's a little weird," she said, tapping her lower lip with the point of her pencil.

Roberta, known to the hospital staff as "Bobs," glanced up from her own paperwork. "What is?"

"There's a girl in the waiting room who's holding her stomach exactly the way Will did right before he collapsed. Think it's something contagious?" Susannah remembered the nasty virus that had swept the city the previous summer. A new strain, brought to Grant from South America. People had *died*. Her twin had almost been one of those people. It had been a scary time for all of Grant. That terrible virus hadn't returned, had it?

"Nope, not contagious," Bobs answered emphatically. "Summer complaint, that's all." She was a big woman, sturdy and strong, with perfect ivory skin and warm brown hair, neatly fastened behind her ears. Patsy Keene and Bobs often worked together. Patsy, small and blond and blue-eyed, was the prettier of the two. But Susannah liked Bobs better. She had a quiet air of competence about her, and her brown eyes twinkled. She performed her duties with dedication and efficiency, and often joked that she had "no life" outside of Med Center. Patsy did, too, but everyone knew she was kidding. She led a very active social life. The running joke in E.R. was, when Patsy Keene had dated every male doctor, orderly, and nurse at Emsee, she'd have to quit and move on to fresh hunting grounds.

Susannah liked both nurses, and was always glad to share a duty roster with them. "Summer complaint? What's that?"

"Oh, you know, that vague ailment that sends people in here in droves when the weather warms. It's the change of season, change in habits, and the excitement of a holiday weekend. Too much sun, too much exercise after a lazy winter, too much food at picnics. They'll be coming in with headaches and upset stomachs."

"So, what do we do for them?"

"Give them capsules for the headache, the gooey pink stuff for the stomachache. I had O'Connor call Grant Pharmaceuticals and stock us up with plenty of both. Fortunately, they're right next door, so if we run out, we can always send someone for more. We give our patients what they need, and then we send them home to recuperate."

It sounded so simple, so cut-and-dried. Nothing major, no big emergency, no life-threatening illness like last summer. "Summer complaint" sounded harmless, no more serious than a minor cut or a low-grade fever.

But, remembering the look of pain on Will's face just before he collapsed, Susannah thought that Will's ailment *must* be serious.

Then five young victims of a boating accident were brought in by dual ambulances, and in the rush to treat them, Susannah forgot about Will and his "summer complaint."

It was a nasty accident. The Revere River, wide and deep, meandered through the city of Grant. Snakelike, it curved and wound its way around narrow peninsulas and small islands. Speeding on such a convoluted waterway was foolish, but it happened.

"If people weren't foolish," Astrid had told Susannah and Kate, "Med Center wouldn't be half as busy as it is."

Drinking had been involved in this particular accident. There were broken limbs, including a compound fracture of a young man's right leg. There were two serious head injuries that required immediate CAT scans to determine the amount of bleeding, if any, in the brain. All five patients had serious bruising and lacerations, and a sixteen-year-old girl had suffered a punctured lung. A chest tube was inserted, and she was transported immediately to the Cardiopulmonary hospital on the grounds.

No one had been killed in the crash.

Gurneys were rushed back and forth, to other buildings in the complex or upstairs to surgery or to one of the cubicles.

"They were lucky," Nurse Patsy Keene commented grimly when the last patient had been treated and wheeled upstairs for overnight observation. "According to the police, they were speeding *and* drinking and went aground on one of the peninsulas. No trees on it, fortunately. If they'd slammed into a tree, they'd all be dead."

When Susannah returned to the waiting room, Julie Whittier was gone.

The elderly man with "heart palpitations" was still there, reading a magazine. Susannah knew him well. His name was Jacob Carson. He lived alone. Whenever loneliness overwhelmed him, he took a taxi to the hospital, complaining of "palpitations." The staff gave him a placebo, which was nothing more than a harmless sugar pill, and sent him home. But unless they were really rushed, they took their time about it, chatting with the old man about world events and politics as long as they possibly could, giving him the attention he craved. Except for very hectic periods when they had no choice but to hurry the elderly man through the routine, he left satisfied.

"Where did the red-haired girl go?" Susannah asked him. "The one with the stomachache?"

Mr. Carson waved a hand toward the restroom out in the corridor.

"She's in there?"

He nodded.

Susannah hurried to the restroom and went inside. "Miss Whittier? Julie Whittier? Are you in here? It's Susannah Grant. We're ready for you now."

No answer. The room appeared to be empty.

Susannah was about to round a corner and check the powder room area when the door behind her burst open, and Abby entered. Her round face was flushed with exertion, her pink smock damp. She was carrying a pail filled with soapy water. "Hey, Sooz, what's up? Gotta wash my hands. I never realized how messy migraine headaches can be. I heard about the boating accident. Didn't lose anyone, did we?"

"No." Susannah moved forward to check the room more thoroughly. "You haven't seen a girl, fifteen or so, with really short, straight red hair, have you? She was in the waiting room, and now I can't find her."

"No, why?" Abby asked. She set the blue plastic pail on the tile floor and moved to the sink. "Losing patients, Susannah? Awfully careless of you. And you made fun of *me* for forgetting my smock."

Susannah stood in the middle of the narrow, white-tiled room, glancing around as if she expected the missing patient to pop up in front of her at any second. "I wonder if she changed her mind and went home? Maybe she was feeling better. But she looked so sick . . . "

A faint groan brought Susannah's head up. "Did you hear that?"

Abby had been running water in the sink. "Hear what?"

It came again, low and dull. Susannah moved around the corner then, to a smaller area that contained a black leather bench, a matching chair, and a long, narrow, metal shelf under a large mirror.

Julie Whittier was lying on the bench. Her hands were pressing against her stomach, her knees were drawn up in pain, and her face was twisted in agony.

Just like Will when he was lying on the track in the stadium.

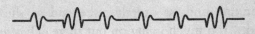

"**A**bby!" Susannah shouted, dropping to a crouch beside the stricken young woman. "Get an orderly and a gurney! Hurry!"

Abby's head appeared around the corner. "What's happening? Oh, my god, it's Julie Whittier. She looks awful! What's wrong with her? She goes to my school. She's on the track team."

"Get some help, Abby!"

Abby disappeared.

Susannah felt for a pulse. When she found it, it seemed steady. The girl's skin was moist and clammy, her eyes tightly closed, her mouth clenched in pain. Her breathing seemed normal, but it was hard to tell because of the way she was doubled up on the bench.

When Susannah asked, "What hurts?" Julie clutched her stomach.

Also just like Will, Susannah thought. Bobs had said that "summer complaint" wasn't contagious. So maybe this was something else . . . a "bug," one of those twenty-four-hour viruses that were so common. They saw a lot of that in

31

the E.R., although just as often it turned out to be food poisoning caused by carelessness in the kitchen.

Abby came back in a moment, pushing one of the wheeled carts used to transport patients. "Couldn't find an orderly," she said as she arrived. "Too much going on out there. They're all busy. I guess it's just you and me, kid." Glancing down at the patient, she commented, "She doesn't look very heavy. The two of us should be able to hoist her on up here." She patted the table, covered with a disposable white sheet. "Julie? Can you climb up on the table?"

The patient groaned, drew her knees up further into her chest, and shook her head from side to side.

Abby shrugged. "Okay, then, I guess it's up to us. You take the head, I'll take the feet."

"Be careful," Susannah warned as she moved to one end of the bench to reach down and lift the girl's thin shoulders. "She's really feeling lousy."

When the patient was on the table, her knees still drawn up to her waist, Abby asked, "You think she's got the same thing Will had? Like a bug or something?"

Susannah shook her head as she eased the gurney out of the room. "Bobs called it 'summer complaint.' It's from the sudden change in temperature." Doubt crept into her voice. "I didn't think it was that hot outside. And summer hasn't even started yet, not technically, not until June."

"You think Bobs was wrong?" Abby looked down at the patient again. "I don't know, Susannah, she's awfully smart. What do *you* think it is?"

"I don't have a clue."

"Well, it's not like it's an epidemic, Sooz. Two cases, that's all. And we don't even know that it's the same thing."

Susannah, pulling the gurney rapidly down the corridor toward the treatment rooms, glanced down at the patient again. She was in so much pain, she was nearly biting through her lower lip. Her long, red fingernails dug into the waistband of her white shorts, as if she were trying to root out the cause of her agony. "Whatever it is," Susannah said quietly, "she's a lot worse off than Will was."

Mixed with her sympathy for Julie Whittier was her relief that Will hadn't been as ill. The thought of seeing him in so much pain made Susannah's own stomach roll over.

They ran with the gurney to an empty treatment room, informing Astrid of the problem as they rushed past the nurses' station.

Dr. Margaret Mulgrew arrived seconds later. She took one look at the patient and immediately began calling out orders. "Chest X ray! Arterial blood gases! CBC, urinalysis!" She began gently exploring the patient's abdomen. "It could be appendicitis. I want a blood count, stat! What's her temp?"

"They didn't do all of that for Will," Abby whispered as orderlies and nurses hastened to obey the doctor's orders.

"They didn't need to," Susannah whispered back.

"I had my appendix out a month ago," Julie Whittier whispered.

"Okay, so I was wrong," Dr. Mulgrew said, checking the patient's pupils. "I get three guesses, right? So," she added casually, "the surgery go okay? Who was your surgeon?"

"Dr. Sumner. Joe Sumner," Julie gasped. "He's my grandfather's friend."

"Were there any complications?" the doctor pressed.

"No. I guess not. But I haven't been feeling very well since I got home. Sort of nauseated and headachy, and I'm tired all the time. And now there's this awful pain in my stomach, like something inside is tearing it to shreds."

Susannah and Abby exchanged an uneasy glance. Occasionally, they'd been told, surgeons goofed. Left something inside the patient that they shouldn't have, like a sponge, or screwed up the stitches during the operation. They had heard of surgeons leaving an operation before it was completed, ordering an inexperienced resident to take over. In cases like that, both the surgeon and the hospital could be sued. As far as Susannah and Abby knew, that hadn't happened at Emsee, not while they'd been there. But it could. People made mistakes, and doctors were people.

Suddenly, Julie Whittier gasped, "Oh, God, I can't breathe!"

"Oxygen!" Dr. Mulgrew called, urgency in her voice.

The room came alive then. To Susannah, watching from one side of the room, it seemed as if someone had set the scene on fast-forward. There had been crisp efficiency before, with people and instruments moving at a normal pace. Now hands flew to seize an oxygen mask, to snatch up a plastic IV bag, to insert a needle in the patient's arm. Feet in rubber-soled shoes whispered hurriedly about the room, setting up the IV pole, pulling a red metal crash cart closer to the table, just in case, and collecting necessary medications from the cabinet behind the table. The scene in the small, white-walled room might have appeared chaotic to a passerby, but Susannah knew that even the most insignificant motion had a purpose. It was perfectly timed and choreographed, an intricate dance whose steps they all knew by heart. They also knew that one false step could be the difference between life and death.

The oxygen helped. When Julie Whittier's breathing had stabilized, the doctor, holding one of the patient's hands in hers, asked Susannah to call in an internist from upstairs. "Since it can't be her appendix, I don't know what it is. I don't want to order more X rays without a confab. Someone get me an inside man."

Susannah was familiar with Dr. Mulgrew's terminology. She called neurosurgerons "head cases," orthopedic surgeons "limb-trimmers," cardiologists "heartbreakers" and by "inside man," she meant a specialist in internal medicine. "Confab" meant a consultation with another doctor.

That would be Dr. Lobell, fourth floor. Susannah made the call.

He came immediately. His preliminary diagnosis was severe food poisoning. "She probably ate some tainted chicken salad at a family picnic," he said dismissively.

When he left the room, an orderly accompanied him, pushing the patient on a gurney. Julie Whittier had calmed down slightly. She would be admitted to the fourth floor, with Dr. Lobell as her primary physician.

After they had gone, Dr. Mulgrew looked skeptical. "Food poisoning?" she said under her breath as she stripped off her thin, rubber gloves. "Her hands looked swollen to me. That doesn't happen with food poisoning. And she said she'd been feeling lousy ever since her surgery. I think I'll have a word with Joe Sumner. I just hope," she added wryly, "that the batteries in his hearing aid aren't running low."

Susannah hadn't noticed that Julie Whittier's hands were swollen, probably because she'd been concentrating on the pained expression on her face.

Kate had suggested to Will that maybe he, too, had eaten something he shouldn't have. He'd denied that at first, then had admitted the bagel might have been moldy. Dr. Lobell would probably agree.

But Dr. Mulgrew might not. She might say that Will's bagel had been just fine, and that Julie Whittier hadn't eaten a bite of chicken salad. If that was true, then what *was* wrong with them?

It didn't really matter, did it? Will had already been treated and was home, resting comfortably, Susannah hoped, and Julie was in good hands now, too. She'd be treated and probably released before nightfall.

There were no more cases of food poisoning while Susannah was on duty.

When it was time to sign out, she hated to leave. Saturday night on a holiday weekend was sure to be horrendous. The staff would need every pair of hands they could get. And Will wasn't going to be at Jeremy's party, anyway.

"You go on now," the night nurse who had taken Astrid's place had insisted. Her name was Greta Schwinn. Like Patsy Keene, she was short, but rounder than the slender Patsy, with beautiful velvety brown eyes and thick, braided, dark hair. She had a gentle manner and a sweet smile. The patients loved her, and so did Susannah. "Go and have fun. You're too serious for such a young person. When I was your age, I was never home."

Susannah believed her. Nurse Schwinn, a widow for three years now, looked like the kind of person who would have an active social life. She was comfortable around all kinds of people, and they liked to be around her. Sam and Abby were like that, too. But, Susannah thought as she neatly folded her smock, not me. She envied all of them their ease in social situations.

Still, she would take the night nurse's advice and go to the party. It was a holiday weekend. It was time to celebrate the beginning of summer. The weather was great, her friends would be there, except for Will, and Jeremy was expecting her. Emsee could get along without her just fine.

On the way home, Abby had to stop at the drugstore to pick up a prescription for her father. He had been burned in a recent refinery fire and although he was making steady progress, he was still recuperating.

Susannah, trying to talk herself into a party

mood, decided maybe a new lipstick would help. She was browsing in the cosmetics department when raised voices caught her attention. They seemed to be coming from the rear of the store, near the pharmacy. A mother and daughter, from the sound of it.

"It's just a stupid earache," the younger voice insisted. "Why do I have to stay home? I'll *use* the ear drops, but I am *not* taking those stupid pills. They'll make me sleepy. And I am *going* to Jeremy Barlow's party tonight. I'm not staying home on a Saturday night just because of an earache. What's the point of going to Med Center and getting medicine if you're still going to treat me as if I were sick? Might as well not even *bother* with the ear drops. Why waste your money?"

"Honestly, you can be so difficult, Toni!" A heavy, motherly sigh followed. Then, "Okay, I give. *Don't* take the pills. Suffer. As for that party, we'll see."

A groan. " 'We'll see'? No. I am going, Mother."

There was more muttered grumbling, then the voices faded.

Susannah didn't know anyone named Toni. But Jeremy apparently did.

chapter
5

They left the drugstore, and Susannah dropped Abby off at her house, promising to pick her up at eight. Then she drove up the steep, winding road that led to the mansion.

The paved, circular driveway at the top of Linden Hill was crowded with vehicles: a white florist's van; the caterer's red truck; the green Jeep her father had bought for Paolo, their head gardener; and a hot-pink Buick sedan with a bouquet of brightly colored balloons decorating the door on the driver's side. Susannah recognized it as the logo for her mother's favorite party-planning company. Her father's cranberry Jaguar and her mother's white Cadillac were parked beneath the porte cochere, leaving just enough room for the Benz. Sam's silver van was nowhere in sight. He must still be at Jeremy's, Susannah thought.

Her mother had accomplished a lot since Susannah left Linden Hall earlier that day. The wide front veranda of the huge, stone and white frame house was beautifully decorated with enormous baskets of spring flowers in shades of lavender and pink. There were more inside. Some sat on the white marble floor, others were perched on tables, and when Susannah went through the house to the back terrace, she found still more giant baskets stationed on the wide stone steps and marking a pathway to the white gazebo in the center of the lawn.

Susannah smiled at the thought of how many florists in town must rejoice whenever Caroline Grant announced plans to host a party. They probably held a party of their own, a florists' fest, to celebrate the thought of all that money flowing into their coffers.

There were workmen everywhere, setting up long, portable tables and folding chairs, stringing lights in pastel colors through the linden trees, putting the finishing touches on a huge white tent off to one side, in case of rain.

It's not going to rain, Susannah thought, following the wide flagstone path to the gazebo. My mother would never allow that.

Caroline Grant, in crisp, white, tailored shorts and a yellow-and-white striped silk blouse, was directing Paolo in the placement of yet another enormous basket of flowers. "No, not there, that would be in the way," she was saying calmly. "To the left more. Oh, hello, dear," she said, smiling when she saw Susannah. "Have you come to help? I know what you could do," Caroline suggested. "It is so warm out here. I'm sure all these wonderful people would appreciate a pitcher of cold lemonade. No, Paolo, to the right a little more, please. Could you do that, Susannah? Ask Mary Margaret to make up a batch of fresh lemonade . . . not the frozen, please . . . and bring it out? With glasses, of course."

Susannah hid a smile. Her mother wasn't even asking her to *make* the lemonade. Her idea of Susannah "helping" was simply to give orders to the staff. "Gee, Mom," she said dryly, "I've had a pretty rough day. I don't know if I have the strength to pull that off, but I'll give it a try."

Caroline, concentrating on Paolo's efforts, missed the sarcasm completely. "Oh, I'm sorry you had a difficult day, dear. Do you have plans for the evening? Something fun, I hope?"

"Party at Jeremy's. I'm picking up Abby at eight."

"That's nice." Caroline frowned. "Now, where has Letitia gone? She was here a second ago. I need her opinion on this."

Letitia Simone was the party-planner. She'd done several parties at Linden Hall. Susannah liked her. She was tall and blond, thin and stylish, with a wicked sense of humor. She worked as a lab technician at Grant Pharmaceuticals during the day, but was developing the party-planning business in the hope that eventually she'd be able to quit the lab job. "That way," she had told Susannah and Caroline, "when I get married and have kids, I can work out of my home. No day care, etcetera. That's my plan." She had grinned. "And you both know, planning is my specialty."

She had dated Jeremy's father for a while. They made an attractive couple, both tall and good-looking, and Susannah had hoped it would turn into something. Tish would make a great mother for Jeremy. For anyone. But Dr. Barlow, who had only been back in the world of the singles a little while, was clearly not ready to settle down.

Jeremy hadn't liked Tish either. But then, he'd liked almost no one his father had dated since the divorce became final. No matter how nice Dr. Barlow's female friends had been, Jeremy was barely civil to them. He wasn't ready to give up hope that his mother would return, begging forgiveness and fully prepared to settle back into the routine she'd left behind. Everyone but Jeremy knew that wasn't going to happen.

Now, whenever someone at Med Center mentioned that Tom Barlow had invited her to dinner, anyone who had already had the pleasure would warn, "Beware of Jer!" Patsy Keene, Bobs Swickert, and Greta Schwinn, nurses at Emsee with whom Susannah often worked, had dubbed Jeremy, "Tom's bomb," because of the destruction Jeremy wreaked on his father's relationships.

"Abby wanted to know if you were serving

chicken salad tomorrow," Susannah told her mother. "We've had a couple of cases of food poisoning at Emsee. Dr. Izbecki says the trouble with picnics is, they're always held in warm weather. He says that's dangerous, that food should never be allowed to sit out on a hot day. Too risky."

Caroline frowned and pursed her lips. "But what would be the point of a picnic on a cold day? That would be so unpleasant."

The party-planner arrived then, arms loaded down with pink and lavender blossoms, an over-sized wicker basket dangling from one wrist. "One more," Tish said, smiling a greeting at Susannah, "over there, in the corner near the tent. Then I think that's it. So, Susannah, are you staying to pitch in?"

Before Susannah could answer, her mother said, "No, she's attending a party at Jeremy Barlow's tonight."

The smile left Letitia Simone's thin, tanned face. "A party? Dear little Jeremy must be celebrating," she said bitterly.

"It's not his birthday, is it?" Caroline asked innocently, taking the flowers and the basket. "I thought Jeremy was born in August. I seem to remember Bianca complaining about the heat when she was expecting him."

"No, it's not his birthday," Susannah said, avoiding Letitia's angry eyes. She knew what the woman's bitter words meant. Tish was suggesting that Jeremy might be "celebrating" because he'd sandbagged her relationship with Thomas Barlow.

Susannah felt a sudden urge to defend Jeremy. How could Tish be so sure that Jeremy was to blame? Since when did Dr. Barlow, an authoritative, impressive man, take orders from his son? Maybe he was just using Jeremy as an excuse, when the truth was, he was the one who was tired of the relationship. But she'd never say that to Tish. It would hurt too much. Tish's broken heart, if she had one, was probably still an open wound. It had only been a month. "Dr. Barlow's out of town," Susannah added, "and he gave Jeremy permission to have a party while he was gone."

Tish's finely arched eyebrows rose. "Tom's out of town?" Caroline didn't hear the party-planner add quietly, "I wonder if he went alone," but Susannah did.

Paolo, perspiring heavily, appeared with one of the workers in tow. "John here isn't feeling so hot," he told Caroline apologetically. "Okay if I let him go home?"

Susannah noticed immediately that the young man in denim overalls was pale and sweaty. His dirt-streaked left hand was on his stomach, just as Will's had been.

"Well, yes, of course," Caroline said, though

she was frowning again. "If the man is ill, he can't very well work, can he? We can manage without him. I hope it isn't anything contagious," she said, before turning away to rearrange the flowers in the basket.

She's forgotten that I ever said anything about food poisoning, Susannah thought, irritated. On an impulse, she asked the worker named John, "Your stomach is bothering you? Maybe you should go to Grant Memorial and have it checked out."

He shook his head. "It's just a stomachache," he said. "Something I ate, maybe."

Yeah, well, there's an awful lot of that going around if you ask me, Susannah thought.

John went home, Paolo returned to work, and Susannah left her mother conferring with Letitia, her dark mood evaporated, about how to decorate the gazebo for the best effect.

When she had ordered the requested lemonade, Susannah hurried up the wide, curving staircase to her three-room suite. Maybe, she thought as she slipped out of her shoes, I'll put in a good word for Tish with Jeremy. It was awful about his mother leaving. Susannah couldn't imagine what it would feel like to have your mother walk out the door one day and leave you behind. But maybe it was time for the Barlow family to move on. Jeremy might be a lot happier with someone as nice as Tish in the house.

From the oversized window beside her king-sized canopy bed, Susannah could see most of the city far below, including the eighteen tall and narrow or shorter, wider, redbrick buildings that made up the Med Center complex. She liked to sit on the bed and imagine what might be going on there while she was absent. But she was happiest when she was there in the thick of things.

For the first weekend in a long time, she'd be spending more time off-duty than on. Attending parties instead of helping out with medical emergencies seemed frivolous to Susannah. But she had promised Jeremy, just as she had promised her parents, she would attend the picnic. "All work and no play," her father had warned with a smile, "makes for a dull life."

That had struck Susannah as funnier than her father had intended. Working in E.R. was many things, but it was *never* dull. Not even on slow days. There was always something going on. Every case wasn't life-threatening, of course. But there was always something. . . .

Maybe she'd just take a quick run over there tomorrow morning, check things out, see if they were understaffed. The picnic wouldn't begin until two in the afternoon. She could help out in E.R. for a few hours, and still be back in plenty of time for the holiday festivities. This picnic was her parents' way of showing appreciation to all the faithful employees who worked in the refinery, at Grant Pharmaceuticals, at the University, and at Emsee, all businesses that involved the Grant family. Most of the town came, and everyone always seemed to have a blast.

But it was the decision to spend at least part of the next day at Emsee that lifted Susannah's spirits as she went to take her shower.

Abby's house was chaotic, as always. The five younger siblings were engaged in a raucous game of touch football on the front lawn. Lazybones, the O'Connors' Irish Setter, chased the cat, Tease, in and out of the shrubbery that Abby's mother, Charlie, in shorts and sneakers, was trimming with electric hedge clippers. "This is really Brendan's job," she said when she had greeted Susannah, "but until he's one hundred percent again, I'm stuck with it."

"How is he?" Susannah asked. Abby's father seemed to be making good, steady progress. When asked, he usually answered, "Hangin' in there." But sometimes Susannah saw lines of pain around his mouth and eyes that revealed the truth.

"Brendan's doing better," Abby's mother said in answer to Susannah's inquiry. "His burns are healing nicely." She looked tired, her pretty face lined with tension, her hair carelessly tossed into a ponytail. Taking care of six kids, the kids' grandfather, and an ailing husband was taking its toll on Charlie O'Connor. She was strong and healthy, but even she had her limits. She clipped at the shrubbery silently for a moment, then added optimistically, "Shouldn't be much longer before he's up and around. Personally, I can't wait."

Abby came rushing out of the house just then, and the conversation ended.

Traffic was heavy on Linden Boulevard. People were on their way to holiday celebrations. Cautiously keeping a safe distance between the Benz and the long line of cars in front of her, Susannah said to Abby, "Your mom looks tired."

"I know," Abby replied. "But Dad's a lot better. Mom wants him to try the pain management clinic at the Burn Center. Dr. Izbecki told us it really does a lot of good."

"Good idea. I've heard the same thing." Susannah pulled the Benz into Jeremy's tree-shaded driveway. Sam's van was there, and several other cars, but it was a long, wide driveway and there was plenty of room. "Remember in our classes how Astrid said of all the cases we'd see in the E.R., two kinds of cases would be the worst? Small children with serious injuries, and all burn cases? Then she said the small children usually recovered quickly, but the burn cases didn't. I guess she was right."

"I guess. It's hard, though. Sid helps a lot. Now that he's been discharged from Rehab, he goes over to my house and plays chess with Dad, and helps Mom with the kids. I think it makes him feel useful, and the truth is, he *is* being useful. My mom says she doesn't know what she'd do without him." Abby smiled. "Sid didn't believe it at first, as if he couldn't buy the idea of being useful in a wheelchair. But he believes it now. And I can tell he likes it."

When they were inside Jeremy's house, its enormous rooms decorated in chrome and glass, the walls white, the floors glossy black tile, the first thing Susannah did was glance around the enormous living room for some sign of the girl from the drugstore, the one who had an earache but insisted on attending Jeremy's party, anyway. She wouldn't be hard to find. Susannah knew all of Jeremy's friends *except* someone named Toni.

When she didn't see anyone unfamiliar, Susannah wondered if the earache had grown worse, wrecking the girl's party plans. That would mean the pills recommended by Mother-knows-best hadn't worked, after all. Or Toni hadn't taken them.

Then Jeremy's voice rang out from the foyer, "Hey, Toni, you made it. Great!"

Susannah turned around.

The girl Susannah had overheard in the drug-store complaining of an earache looked perfectly healthy. "Toni" was a tall, thin girl with light brown hair tied up underneath a red baseball cap. She greeted Jeremy with a grin and a careless wave of a hand. Susannah had expected her to look pale, but the girl's face was sunburned, giving her a healthy glow.

The eardrops must have worked.

Other party guests began to arrive, noisily spilling into the spacious foyer. Among them was Callie Matthews, whose father Caleb ran Med Center.

Callie looked like a Christmas tree. She was overdressed, as always. In the midst of shorts and jeans and tank tops and a few pastel-colored slip dresses, she was wearing a green taffeta strapless dress and green high heels. Her blond waves were piled on top of her head, her blue eyes heavily outlined with black pencil, her small, oval, slightly pinched face layered with makeup.

Like a cake with too much frosting, Susannah

thought. Why doesn't her mother help her get ready for these things? Callie's mother was a semi-invalid, chronically ill with kidney disease. But Susannah knew that when Mrs. Matthews did go out on rare occasions, she always looked beautiful, her clothes and jewelry elegant, her makeup tastefully done. Was she too ill to give her seventeen-year-old daughter advice?

Callie's going to ask me if Sam is here yet, Susannah predicted with certainty.

"Is Sam here yet?" Callie asked anxiously.

"I don't know. I just got here."

Callie tossed her head and hurried away, in search of Sam.

Susannah followed, wondering where Abby was.

She found her with Jeremy in the living room, a wide, deep space with high ceilings and enormous windows, uncurtained, looking out over the beautifully landscaped grounds. The floor was hardwood, perfect for dancing. There were tables situated under the windows. One held bowls of chips and dip and an ice bucket surrounded by stacks of paper cups. The other was laden with a dozen or more trays of food, which Susannah knew the housekeeper had prepared for Jeremy.

The music playing was soft, romantic. Abby, who had decided on the green outfit, a pair of gauzy palazzo pants and a long-sleeved, scoop-neck blouse, was already dancing. She was seated on Sid's lap, her arms around his neck; he spun his wheelchair around expertly. Jeremy, as overdressed as Callie in a white shirt and tie under a tweed blazer that had to be too warm for the weather, was sitting on the stone fireplace hearth, his chin in his hands. His blond hair was neatly combed, as always, his square, attractive face solemn.

Susannah made her way through half a dozen dancing couples and sat down beside him. "This is not a party face I see," she said with mock sternness. "People seem to be having a good time. Why so glum?"

Jeremy didn't look up. "My dad just called. He's not coming home tomorrow, like he was supposed to. He's in Palm Springs, and he said the weather's so good, he's decided to stay and do some golfing." Jeremy scowled. "But that's not the *real* reason he's staying. It's that *woman*."

"What woman?" Susannah thought of Tish. Had Tish's fears been justified? Had Dr. Barlow taken someone with him to Palm Springs?

"Some doctor he met at the convention. From Schenectady, New York. I can't remember her name. He sounded like he really liked her, though."

You don't *want* to remember her name, Susannah thought. As for Tish, she wouldn't be comforted to learn that Dr. Barlow had gone to the convention alone, but had met someone while he was there.

"When he left," Jeremy said angrily, "he promised me he'd be back tomorrow. He said we'd play tennis at the club, then go to your parents' picnic, make a day of it. I should have known it wouldn't happen. Something always comes up."

Jeremy would wallow in his misery all night if someone didn't snap him out of it. "That girl Toni seems nice," Susannah said, deliberately changing the subject. "Where did you meet her?"

"At the library on Tuesday. How's Will?"

"Okay, I guess. We had another case like his later on, much worse, so maybe it's a bug. Why don't you ask her to dance?"

"Who?"

Susannah laughed. "Toni, you dimwit! Isn't that who we were talking about? Go on, Jeremy. Dance. Have fun. This is a party, not a wake! You and your dad can golf next weekend. Anyway, plenty of people you know will be at the picnic. Bring Toni, if you want. The more, the merrier."

That seemed to work. Jeremy sighed heavily, but he stood up and went to fetch Toni, who was standing beside the food table, heaping a paper plate high.

I guess her earache hasn't affected her appetite,

Susannah thought as she surveyed the room for her brother. Sam should be around somewhere, if Callie hadn't already whisked him away to her lair.

Susannah found herself wishing that Kate and Damon were coming. But Damon, a fireman, was on duty until midnight, and Kate had decided to stay home and study for finals. She kept insisting that Damon was just a friend, but Susannah was positive that wasn't true. She'd seen the look on Kate's face when Damon had narrowly escaped being caught in a cave-in. He'd been working to rescue people trapped in a building that had collapsed, and Kate had been frantic. That was more than just a friendship, in spite of what Kate said.

Parties were more fun with Kate.

When Susannah found her brother, she was surprised to see tall, lovely, Lily Dolan at his side. Not only were they together, Sam had his arm around Lily and looked quite content. So did Lily. She had changed from her nurse's aide uniform into a flowered skirt and white tank top. Her wildly curly auburn hair was caught up in a ponytail. She was smiling up at Sam, and she looked beautiful.

Susannah walked over to them. "Hey, you both made it, that's great." She smiled at Lily. "I wasn't sure you'd be able to come."

"Neither was Callie," Lily said dryly. "You should have seen the look on her face when I walked in."

Susannah's smile widened. "I wouldn't be surprised to see smoke pouring out of her ears. You'd be smart to steer clear of her, or she might spoil your fun."

"No problem," Sam agreed. "That's something I would have done even if Lily hadn't showed up. But," smiling down at Lily, "I'm glad she did. You'll protect me from Callie, won't you?"

Lily shook her head negatively. "I can't. I didn't bring my pesticide."

Sam laughed.

"Well, look who's here!" Susannah heard Abby cry out. "I thought you weren't coming." But when Susannah turned around, Abby wasn't looking at Sam and Lily. Her eyes were on the door.

Susannah followed her gaze. Will, in jeans and a white shirt with the sleeves rolled up to the elbow, was standing in the doorway. His eyes met hers, and he smiled at the look of delighted surprise on her face. She hurried toward him, the spring in her step emphasizing how glad she was to see him.

"You must be feeling better," she said when she reached him.

Without a word, he took her hand and led her

out into the middle of the floor, pulled her close to his chest, and began dancing.

When the song ended, she lifted her head. "So, *are* you? Feeling better?"

"Yep. The pink goo Izbecki gave me worked. I figured there was no point in wasting a perfectly good Saturday night. Holiday weekend and all that, know what I'm sayin'?"

Susannah was surprised at how Will's arrival had improved her mood. Now that he was here, holding her hand and smiling down at her, she felt lighter, as if she were floating. She felt the way Sam and Lily looked. Content. Everything was better when she shared it with Will.

He got them both something to drink and led her out onto the back terrace. There were other couples enjoying the balmy night, dancing on the flagstones or sitting on one of the stone benches, talking or eating from paper plates. As they settled on a stone bench on the sloping back lawn, away from the people gathered on the terrace, Callie Matthews's thin, high voice assailed their ears.

"Callie, are you *following* us?" Susannah asked irritably. "Get a life! It's tragic that you don't have anything better to do."

"Well, I thought I would tonight," Callie grumbled, tossing her head. The too-sophisticated upsweep teetered precariously. "I thought Sam was coming alone. I had plenty of chances for a date tonight, *plenty*." Her voice became even more nasal. "But I felt sorry for Sam, coming all by himself, so I turned down all my other invitations. Now I don't have anyone to dance with, except Jeremy, and he's hovering over that weird girl."

"Toni. That 'weird girl's' name is Toni. I think she's cute."

"She's crazy. She is actually sliding down the stair railing, like a stupid six-year-old. And she's too loud. She practically shrieks everything. She sounds like the refinery whistle. And I don't *care* what her name is." Callie plopped down on the bench beside Susannah. "She's not Jeremy's type at all. I heard she's some kind of artist or something. She certainly doesn't know the first thing about fashion."

This from someone wearing green taffeta, Susannah thought. "If she's an artist," she said aloud, "they do have something in common. Jeremy's artistic." Jeremy's interest in art was something Dr. Barlow refused to acknowledge. He was determined that Jeremy would go into medicine, though Jeremy had no interest in the field. If Toni really was an artist, maybe she'd encourage Jeremy to follow his own heart instead of his father's wishes.

"Everyone has someone but me," Callie whined.

Susannah almost felt sorry for her. Then she remembered all the times in the past when Callie's meanness had caused so much trouble for so many people, and her heart hardened. "You just said you could have had a date," she said unsympathetically. "It's your own fault you're alone. Sam's with Lily now, Callie. Give it up. Find someone else."

"I don't *want* someone else! I want Sam. I've always wanted Sam. And I'm *not* giving up! Ever!" Fuming, Callie jumped up and flounced off.

"That girl is hazardous to *everyone's* health," Will commented, returning an arm to Susannah's shoulders and gently pulling her close to his chest again. "If I were Sam, I'd steer clear of her. Jeremy, too."

"If I were *Lily*, I'd steer clear of her," Susannah said grimly. "Callie would never hurt Sam or Jeremy. It's Lily she wants out of the way. It's a good thing Lily Dolan can take care of herself. She didn't let her father push her around, and she's certainly not going to let Callie Matthews do it, either."

"Hey," Will said softly, reaching up to turn Susannah's face toward his. "Where were we when Callie showed up?"

"We were here," she said, lifting her face to his.

Moments later, it was Abby's voice that

snapped both of them back to reality. She was shouting from the back terrace, and she sounded frantic. "Susannah! Get in here! Jeremy's date fell off the stair railing. She's hurt, and I don't know what to do!"

chapter
7

Abby was even more panic-stricken than her voice suggested. It was as if her mind had been vacuumed free of everything she'd learned in her volunteer classes.

She'd been sitting on the fireplace hearth with Sid, her black flats off, her stockinged feet tucked up underneath her dark green skirt. Everyone was talking, laughing, listening to great music and eating from paper plates. They were all watching with amusement as Toni, Jeremy's date, slid down the shiny, slippery, oak stair railing, laughing as she jumped to safety at the bottom of the wide, carpeted stairs. Then she ran back up, her long legs taking the stairs two at a time, to do it again. She had made the trip half a dozen times without incident.

Then suddenly, without warning, she cried out, clutched at her stomach, lost her balance, and toppled over the side, arms flailing. She had just started down, and the stairs were steep, giving her a long distance to fall. She landed face-down on the hardwood floor. When her forehead collided with the floor, there was a startling, "thwacking" sound. Toni let out a grunt, and her eyes slammed shut.

People jumped to their feet. Paper plates fell to the floor, spilling food. Feet rushed to the bottom of the stairs.

"Abby?" Jeremy called, his eyes on the crumpled form at his feet.

Abby knew why Jeremy had instinctively called out *her* name. Because she worked at Emsee. He expected her to know what to do. But . . . she worked mostly in Rehab, not in Emergency like Susannah. And this was clearly an emergency. Toni was unconscious.

Abby's mind went blank. She couldn't think of a single thing she should be doing for the stricken girl. Jeremy, staring down at Toni in shock, didn't know what to do, either. He should have done something sooner, he thought guiltily. *He* had never been allowed to slide down the stair railing. His father would have been very angry if he'd seen Toni doing it.

Maybe that was *why* he'd let her do it. Because it would have made his father nuts. Jeremy felt even guiltier. He should have stopped her.

"Is she dead?" he asked Abby in a hoarse whisper.

"No. Get Lily. She's a nurse's aide. She'll know what to do."

"She's not in here," Sid said. He wheeled his

chair over, stopping when he reached Abby and Jeremy. "She went for a walk with Sam. I'll go get them."

"No, I'll go," Abby cried without thinking. "It'll be faster." She didn't see the look on Sid's face as she turned and ran for the back door. Jeremy did, but he couldn't worry about Sid's feelings now, not with Toni lying unconscious at his feet. He had a feeling Abby would find Sid in a totally different mood when she came back. Sid's face was white, his mouth tense. Abby had hurt his feelings, Jeremy realized, even though she hadn't meant to, even though she was right. Her flying feet *would* be faster than Sid's wheelchair. But if she hadn't been upset and anxious about Toni, she never would have pointed that out to Sid.

Jeremy knelt beside the unconscious girl, took her hand in one of his, and then didn't know what to do with it. Take her pulse, he guessed. But he was afraid to. What if it wasn't there? Abby could be mistaken. She wasn't a doctor. That awful sound when Toni landed . . . she *could* be dead.

What had happened? She'd been fine only a moment before, laughing and clearly loving being the center of so much attention. He'd been thinking that although she was very different from any girl he'd ever dated before, he liked her. He'd actually been having a good time, something that didn't always happen for him at parties, especially his own.

Toni was wild and crazy and fun, and she knew a lot about art, something he'd always been interested in. She'd mentioned having an earache earlier that day, but had said she was feeling fine, and the way she'd been dancing up a storm with him, he'd believed her.

So why was she lying on the floor, her eyes closed, her mouth open in surprise, as if she didn't know any more than he did what had happened to her?

"Abby, hurry up!" he shouted over his shoulder.

When Abby came rushing back into the room, Lily wasn't with her. But Susannah and Will were. Jeremy went weak with relief. They'd know what to do to keep Toni from dying.

"How is she?" Susannah asked as they arrived. She knelt beside the girl, lifted her wrist to take her pulse. "How's her breathing?"

Will motioned the crowd away from Toni. "Jeremy, get these people back, so the girl will have some air." Then he knelt to listen to Toni's chest. "She's breathing," he announced.

Jeremy sank back on his heels. She was breathing. She was alive.

"Anyone call an ambulance?" Will asked.

A girl called out, "I did. They're on their way."

"Good." Lowering his voice, Will said to Susannah, "I wish I had my jump bag." He was referring to the equipment bag carried on all ambulances. "We should be checking her blood pressure. She could have internal injuries." He asked Jeremy, "How far did she fall?"

"Too far." Jeremy pointed to the railing. "She wasn't far from the top of the stairs when she toppled over. She fell away from the stairs instead of onto them. Landed on her forehead, hard. That's what knocked her out."

Will nodded. "She's out, all right. But she might not be seriously hurt."

Susannah, still holding Toni's wrist, asked Jeremy quietly, "Why do you think she fell?"

He shook his head. "I don't know. She'd already done it five or six times, no problem. But this time, she yelled, sort of like she was in pain, and I think she grabbed her stomach." His eyes moved to Will. "Like you, today at the track. Then she fell."

"She had an earache earlier today," Susannah said. "Not a stomachache. An earache. I heard her talking about it in the drugstore. Are you sure it was her stomach she grabbed?"

"Of course I'm sure," Jeremy said irritably. "But it wasn't the food she ate here. It couldn't have been. We *all* ate the same stuff, and no one else is complaining."

"So *far*," Callie said from behind him. "I'm not touching another morsel on that table. We

65

should tell the paramedics to take samples of everything we ate, for testing at the lab, just in case it's got some horrible bacteria in it or something."

Jeremy paled visibly. "It wasn't the food," he insisted.

"I'm with you," Will agreed. His eyes moved again to the stricken girl. "If she really did look the same way I did at the track, it couldn't be the food here, because I never ate any of it, right? Relax, Jeremy. If she *did* have a stomachache, your party food didn't cause it."

Jeremy turned to direct a baleful glance in Callie's direction. She ignored it.

Susannah sent Jeremy upstairs for a blanket to cover Toni. Grateful to be given something to do, Jeremy ran upstairs, returning a moment later with an armful of pastel-colored blankets.

Susannah had just covered the patient when the ambulance arrived.

The party ended quickly. Jeremy announced his intention of following his ailing party guest to Med Center. Others did the same, including Lily and Sam, who were visibly shocked when they returned to the party to find paramedics there.

While the medical personnel checked out the patient, Jeremy apologized to all of his guests for cutting the evening short.

"Oh, get real, Jeremy," Callie said, tossing a green taffeta wrap around her bare shoulders.

She was totally disgusted by the way Sam was practically welded to Lily. Not about to attack Sam, she switched her anger to Jeremy, an easier target. "You don't really think anyone would want to stay here and party *now*, do you? We could all end up just like that crazy girl!"

Jeremy reddened with anger, but said nothing.

Will stood up, letting the other paramedics handle the patient. "I told you, Callie," he said patiently but firmly, "nothing at this party made this girl sick. It has to be something else."

Callie laughed rudely. "Oh, right, *Doctor* Jackson! Like *you* would know. Excuse *me*, but I don't think there's an M.D. after your name just yet, is there?"

Jeremy surprised everyone in the room then by saying heatedly, "Oh, why don't you just shut up, Callie? We've got enough problems here right now. You don't care about Toni, so why don't you just go home and count your shoes or something?"

Callie's face flamed. She knew no one would miss her.

She had had a horrible evening. Being the only one without a date was humiliating. When Lily Dolan had shown up with Sam, she'd known this party was going to be a dud. *Worse* than that, even.

"I don't like it when people treat me like this," Callie retorted, her eyes narrowing. She was addressing Jeremy, but her eyes were on Sam as he helped the paramedics gently lift Toni onto a stretcher. "I thought you already knew that about me, Jeremy." That said, she turned and stalked away, her high heels clicking across the hardwood floor. At the door, she turned dramatically and bit off the words, "By the way, you give a really lousy party." Then she slammed the front door hard.

"Sounds like you made the lady mad," one of the paramedics said as he and his partner, carrying Toni on a stretcher, passed Jeremy.

Jeremy shrugged. "Yeah, well, that's nothing new." Then he asked anxiously, "How is Toni? Is she going to be okay?" He stayed close to the stretcher.

"I think so. No real problem with her vital signs. Might have a concussion, though. Got a lump the size of a bowling ball on her forehead."

Susannah, walking beside Will, murmured, "Jeremy said he thought her stomach hurt her. Like you, earlier. But Toni didn't share a bagel with you this morning, am I right? Neither did Julie Whittier."

"Yeah, you're right."

When the ambulance doors had closed, Susannah and Will, Abby and Sid and Jeremy followed in Sam's van. They hardly knew Toni, but they were Jeremy's friends. He looked like he could use some moral support.

The conversation turned, naturally, to food and its dangers.

After a few minutes, Sam made an impatient sound. "Hey, whadya say we talk about something a little more upbeat? This is a holiday weekend, remember?"

"We remember," Abby retorted, "but we also remember that we're on our way to a *hospital*. How upbeat can we be?"

Then they were pulling into Med Center's wide, tree-lined driveway, behind the ambulance. They rushed into the E.R. after the stretcher.

Dr. Cathy Schumann, a short, round, blond resident, was on duty. When Susannah and Abby hurried into Toni's treatment room, an array of tests had already been ordered, including chest X ray, glucose tests, and arterial blood gases. The patient was conscious, but quiet. A nurse was taking her blood pressure, and Dr. Schumann was examining the egg-sized lump on Toni's forehead.

"Someone said they thought she had a stomachache just before she fell off the railing," Susannah said, thinking of Will, and Julie Whittier. "We had a couple of cases of food poisoning in here earlier. Think this is the same thing?"

"Well, it's not salmonella," the doctor answered. "We took her temp. No fever. But I guess it could be some other organism. Could be staph . . . staphylococcus. If it is, it won't last more than a few hours. But there are more serious organisms, too. We won't know anything for sure until the lab tests come back. In the meantime, I'm sending this one upstairs to Lobell. He's still on the floor, and he can compare this case to the one he had earlier today. You said there were *two* cases?"

Susannah nodded. "Sort of. I mean, Will Jackson was the first one, but he wasn't nearly as sick as the second case, Julie Whittier. If she had the same thing. She's the one we sent upstairs with Lobell."

"Right. She hasn't been discharged yet."

That surprised Susannah. Dr. Schumann had just said that a simple case of food poisoning might only last a few hours. Julie had already been in the hospital since early that afternoon. Didn't that indicate that her case was *not* so simple? That it really could be a result of a screwed-up appendectomy?

Stupid to worry about Julie Whittier now. Jeremy was upset about Toni. When Dr. Schumann had made her diagnosis, she would probably expect Susannah to go with her to inform Jeremy. She was, after all, his friend.

Unless Toni was in better shape than she appeared to be, Susannah wasn't looking forward to that conversation.

chapter

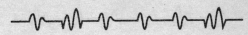

It's happening. But so slowly. Was I too careful? It would be much more interesting if people were falling like dominoes. More fun, too.

But then it would have been finished too soon. That's not the way I planned it.

There won't be a real scandal involving Med Center unless someone dies. Maybe Whittier will. That would be a bonus, because she just had surgery. If she dies, it'll be blamed on some inept surgeon. Then they won't bother looking for any other cause. Perfect. That'll give me extra time. And more victims.

Slow is better, after all. Safer.

It's happening.

I only wish they could all know who is behind their ruin.

Especially him.

chapter
9

Susannah did tell Jeremy that Toni had been taken upstairs. But that was all she could tell him. No test results had come back from the lab.

"They're awfully busy," she apologized. "You should probably go home. I can call you if I find out anything more tonight."

He shook his head. "I'll stay. I need to hear a doctor say it isn't food poisoning." He glared at Callie, who had followed them to the hospital. "So does Callie, before she goes to the newspapers with a story that Jeremy Barlow's parties send people to the E.R."

Callie tossed her head.

Sam, deciding he couldn't be of any help, left with Lily and Sid.

Susannah, seeing how busy the E.R. was, decided to stay. Will wanted to stay, too, thinking that as a paramedic, he might be able to help out. But Dr. Izbecki vetoed that idea. "There's still a chance that you're coming down with something, Jackson. Go home, get some sleep, see how you feel tomorrow."

Will left Emsee reluctantly, after asking Susannah to call him later and let him know how things were going.

Abby decided to stay, too.

"The party's over, anyway," she said as she and Susannah went in search of the night nurse, Greta Schwinn. "It's not that late. I can hang around for a while. I want to see how Toni is doing."

Susannah nodded. "Me, too. I hope she's not as sick as Julie Whittier. Schumann told me Julie hasn't been discharged yet. She's still upstairs."

"Well, she did look pretty awful. Her skin was so yellowish. Weird."

The air of tension in the E.R. had increased considerably. No one was relaxing in the staff lounge, there didn't seem to be an empty gurney anywhere, and the odor of medication hung heavy in the air.

"We've had a bunch of car wrecks," Greta Schwinn told them when they located her in one of the treatment rooms. She was hastily restocking a cabinet with medical supplies. "Another near-drowning . . . the kid was full of muddy water from the Revere, but we pumped it out of him. Those two migraine patients Astrid told me about were back, this time complaining of stomach pains. We medicated them and sent them home."

Susannah was relieved. This time, the stomachache cases hadn't been severe. The two migraine patients were luckier than Julie and Toni. "Anything else?"

"Two boys burned by firecrackers. Fooling around. One nearly lost a hand. He's in surgery as we speak. The other one has a burn under one eye. He came very close to losing his sight, but he seemed to think a scar would be really cool."

"Sounds like you've had your hands full," Abby said. "Can you use four more?"

Nurse Schwinn looked blank. "Four more what?"

Abby laughed. "Four more *hands*!" Then she held out the edges of her dark green tunic. "If we can work without smocks. We didn't bring them."

"You can work stark naked for all I care," Nurse Schwinn said gratefully. "Of course I can use you. In a dozen places at the same time. And you can borrow lab coats if you're worried about your clothes."

"Have you heard anything about Julie Whittier's condition?" Susannah asked as they all began walking back to the nurses' station. "Is she any better?"

Greta Schwinn's full pink lips clamped shut. "I'm not at liberty to discuss that case," she said.

Her expression and tone of voice were so unlike her usual demeanor, Susannah thought at first that she was kidding. When she realized that the head nurse was serious, she thought, Uh-oh, what's going on? "Not at liberty to discuss"? What did *that* mean?

"Something's going on," she told Abby in a hushed voice as, in borrowed white lab coats, they left to take up their stations. Susannah was headed for a suture room. Abby, who wasn't permitted in the cubicles, had been assigned to the waiting room. "I've been working here for almost a year now, and this is the first time one of the nurses has refused to discuss a case. It's weird."

"Julie must be sicker than everybody thought." Abby rolled up the sleeves of the oversized lab coat. "The staff is probably thinking about that terrible virus last summer. Maybe they're afraid if the word gets out, everyone in Grant will panic."

The explanation made sense. But as the two girls separated in the peach-walled corridor, Susannah couldn't help thinking of a second possible explanation. Julie Whittier had recently undergone surgery at Med Center. Her appendix had been removed. Now here she was, back in the hospital again, and seriously ill. Dr. Lincoln had been skeptical about Dr. Lobell's diagnosis of "food poisoning." And Nurse Schwinn had been ordered not to discuss the case. Did the hospital administrators now suspect that one of the surgeons at Emsee had made a serious error during Julie Whittier's surgery? That would explain why Nurse Schwinn's lips had been sealed.

Susannah entered the suture room. Dr. Izbecki was carefully stitching up a deep laceration on the left arm of a ten-year-old boy who'd climbed a utility pole to get a better look at the fireworks display, and had fallen. His white-faced mother was standing beside the table, holding the boy's free hand. Parents were only allowed in an emergency treatment cubicle if the injury wasn't life-threatening and if they remained calm. At the first sign of panic, they were quickly escorted from the area. This woman, tall and thin, in white, bloodstained shorts and white T-shirt, seemed to be holding up well. The boy, thanks to a numbing injection to the wound area, made no sound.

There was little for Susannah to do beyond holding the suture tray which, because the nurses were all busy, Dr. Izbecki had propped on his knee.

Watching the doctor's neat, expert stitches wind their way up the freckled arm, Susannah hoped fiercely that her explanation for Nurse Schwinn's silence was totally wrong. She preferred Abby's theory: a fear of panic. That was so much more palatable. A surgeon's serious mistake would be bad for the hospital, for the entire Med Center complex . . . not to mention for Julie Whittier. "Summer complaint" was no big deal. But a sponge or a gauze pad, any foreign object, no matter how small, accidentally left inside an incision, if gone undetected for too long, was a *very* big deal. It would cause infection, could even cause death.

Abby had to be right. Julie was ill with some kind of flu or nasty little bug, and the hospital staff was simply being cautious, fearing panic because of last summer's fatalities. Perfectly understandable, when you thought about it. Good thinking. Who needed panic on an already hectic holiday weekend?

When Susannah left the suture room, she felt calmer. And she felt even better when Kate's smiling face appeared around a corner.

Susannah waved. "I thought you were studying!"

"I'm psychic," Kate answered, moving out into the corridor. "I had this vision that you needed me here. I heard voices calling, 'Kate! Kate! E.R. is rocking with activity! Get your buns over here right now, before the place goes up in smoke!' " She grinned. "So here I am!"

She was wearing jeans and a blue-and-green short dashiki she had made.

"Funny you never mentioned this amazing gift of yours before," Susannah said dryly. She had noticed Damon Lawrence, still wearing his black fireman's helmet, leaning against the wall outside of one of the treatment rooms when she was looking for the head nurse. "Your sudden appearance here wouldn't have anything to do with all those grass fires started by firecrackers, would it? And a certain gorgeous fireman?"

Kate's beautiful face took on an expression of mock wounded pride. "Susannah Grant! Are you questioning my dedication to this great institution of healing? When I have sacrificed my free time and relentlessly worked my fingers to the bone?" She lowered her voice then and asked in a conspiratorial tone, "So, where *is* he?"

Susannah laughed.

"I know he's here," Kate continued. "I heard on the radio that a couple of kids with sparklers started a grass fire on the riverbank in the West End. The announcer said one of them had been burned. I knew if Damon was on the call, he'd still be here, waiting to see if the kid was okay. But," she added quickly, "that's *not* why I came. I called here *before* I heard that news report, and Schwinn said things were really wild. I'd already decided to pitch in when I heard about those kids."

"Treatment room six," Susannah finally said.

Kate turned and hurried away, calling over her shoulder, "Be right back! I just want to tell him hi."

Susannah watched her go with a smile. No matter what Kate said about "just being friends" with Damon, she had an eagerness in her steps that said otherwise. Her "hi" to Damon might take more than a minute.

Susannah decided to fill the time by checking every treatment room, and moved on into the one closest to her.

When Abby walked into the crowded E.R. waiting room, she gravitated immediately toward a little boy she recognized. His name was Bradley Duval. He had blond, very curly hair and enormous brown eyes. He was sitting on his mother's lap, his face twisted as he fought valiantly not to cry. One hand rubbed the denim jeans covering his rounded belly.

His mother, an attractive woman in an elegant yellow suit, stroked his forehead, speaking to her son in a soft, soothing voice.

Although Abby spent far less time in E.R. than Susannah, she had seen Bradley Duval arrive in E.R. three times in the past year. The first time, he'd broken his left wrist in a fall from the jungle gym at a park near his house. The little boy's bravery had impressed her. He hadn't let out so much as a whimper throughout his treatment.

The second time, his father, a tall, man in a well-tailored gray suit, brought his son in with a head injury suffered in another fall, this one from an upper bunk bed. "He must have hit his head on one of the wheels."

Dr. Helene Maclaine, the pediatrician treating the boy, had frowned and said, "His bed has wheels?"

Mr. Duval had smiled and answered, "Both bunks are replicas of sportscars. My wife's idea. I was concerned about the wheels initially. But Beth, my wife, assured me they were perfectly safe, as did the builder."

That second time, the blow to the little boy's skull had been severe enough to warrant a CAT scan, to check for bleeding in the brain. The results had been negative, and he'd gone home within twenty-four hours.

Bradley's third admission to the E.R. had taken place on a windy, snowy, winter evening when Abby had agreed to sub for a volunteer who was reluctant to drive on nasty roads. Both parents had accompanied the little boy, and both had hovered over him anxiously during treatment.

This time, when the pediatrician arrived in the cubicle and spotted Bradley on the table, she had snapped, "Is this child accident-prone or is it simply that no one is supervising his activities?"

Abby wasn't surprised. Helene Maclaine was wonderful with her young patients. Gentle and kind and reassuring. The children loved her. But she had far less tolerance for the adults who were responsible for the youngsters' safety. Abby had once overheard her lecture a mother for fifteen minutes because she'd neglected to have her three children inoculated against preventable childhood diseases. "There is a free clinic right next door," Dr. Maclaine had said coldly to the cowering young mother. "You have absolutely no excuse for neglecting these children this way. You take them over there this very afternoon and see about their shots, or I'm calling Social Services."

As for Bradley Duval, three visits from one child in such a short period of time was beyond Dr. Maclaine's tolerance level. "Well?" she demanded when no one answered her question." "What happened?"

Small drops of red trickled from a spot just underneath the little boy's left ear. His left cheek was also painfully red. Although the injury had to be hurting, there was no sign that he'd been crying. He sat silently on the table, his hands in his lap, waiting patiently to see what the doctor was going to do to him this time.

"He was outside playing," Mrs. Duval said, her arm around her son's shoulders. "I was just about to call him inside, afraid he'd catch a chill. I went to the front door, and just as I got there I saw him slip on a patch of ice and fall against the stone birdbath in the front yard, striking his cheek and ear on its edge. I ran right out and picked him up, didn't even bother to put a coat on. It might be just a scratch, but I'd rather be safe than sorry. We brought him right here. I want you to check and make sure there's no damage to the ear itself."

There was at least one problem with that

story, as far as Abby was concerned. Bradley was wearing jeans and a sweater under his black down jacket, and he wasn't wearing boots or gloves or a hat. His jeans weren't wet, nor were his sneakers. If he'd been playing outside, with the snow coming down thick and fast, wouldn't his clothes be wet? His parents would hardly have taken the time to change them before they brought him to E.R.

Abby was having trouble swallowing the story about the birdbath, too. It stuck in her throat like a cold, hard stone.

Dr. Maclaine must have shared her doubts, because she bent close to the boy and asked, "Is that what happened, Bradley?"

And although he nodded and said, "Birdbath," his voice was a dutiful monotone and his eyes were blank.

Dr. Maclaine looked skeptical. She sent the parents out of the room and talked to the little boy alone, pressing him for the truth about what had happened to him.

He would say only, "Birdbath."

Later, when the boy had been treated and sent home, Abby had boldly approached the pediatrician and said, "That mark on his cheek looked like a handprint to me. And this was his third time here."

"I know." Helene Maclaine sighed and shook her head. "But do you know who those people are? Arthur Duval is president of the First National Bank, and his father-in-law is Chairman of the Board of Directors."

Abby's eyebrows met in a frown. "So? Presidents of banks are allowed to smack their kids around?"

"Of course not. But we have no proof of abuse. And the child isn't going to say anything against his parents. I tried. Without his confirmation, we don't dare make accusations."

Abby wasn't willing to give up. "I'll bet you could get something out of him. If you had more time alone with him. You can talk a three-year-old into letting you stick a needle into his arm, so you could probably talk Bradley Duval into telling you what's really happening to him."

"I gave it my best shot, O'Connor." Dr. Maclaine sighed again as she began putting medical instruments away. "Maybe I'll talk to Matthews, see what he thinks. But I happen to know that he golfs with Arthur Duval every Wednesday afternoon, so I'm not very optimistic."

Abby wasn't, either. Caleb Matthews, Callie's father, had always impressed her as the same kind of ambitious, social-climbing fool as his daughter. He wouldn't want to offend a bank president.

She was right. The next time she saw Dr. Maclaine and inquired about the Duvals, the pediatrician shrugged and shook her head.

Now the little boy was back again, sitting in the waiting room with his mother's loving arms around him.

Just how loving were those arms, really?

Her lips pressed tightly together, Abby approached mother and son, wondering what was wrong with Bradley this time.

chapter
10

—⎍⋀⋀⋀⋀⎍—

It took a lot to fire up Abby O'Connor's temper. Small annoyances such as her sister Moira borrowing her best pink silk blouse, wearing it, then tossing it carelessly into a corner, didn't do it. Someone cutting in front of her in traffic brought no more than a disgusted "Jerk!" from her mouth. Even Callie Matthews, who seemed to have made it her life's goal to annoy people, seldom bothered with Abby, knowing how much it took to set her off.

But a child who might be suffering at the hands of his parents heated Abby's blood to a boil.

"What's wrong with Bradley this time?" she asked Mrs. Duval coldly as she reached mother and child.

A quizzical expression appeared on Mrs. Duval's attractive face. "I don't know. He's complaining of a stomachache. We were worried that it might be his appendix, but isn't he awfully young for that?"

"Yes." Abby placed a hand on the child's forehead. No fever. Good. But he was clenching his small, pointed jaw and squeezing his eyes shut against the pain, which must have been fierce. "What has he had to eat today?"

The woman sat up straighter, careful not to disturb the child lying in her lap. "Are you an intern? You don't look old enough."

"No." Abby knelt beside the boy. He was very pale. "I'm a volunteer. I need to get some information from you." She held up her clipboard.

Mrs. Duval cleared her throat. "I'm sure you can understand that I would prefer to speak to a doctor. It's been a very trying day, and I'm too exhausted to answer questions repeatedly. Why have we had to wait so long? Does Dr. Maclaine know we're here?"

"It's a holiday weekend. We're very busy." Dr. Maclaine would never give preferential treatment to someone just because they had money and position. "The doctor will see you as soon as she can. How long has Bradley been like this?"

The woman's mascara had smudged, creating smoky shadows under her eyes. "I would really prefer to discuss all of that with the doctor. Could you please tell her that Bradley is in serious condition?"

Realizing that she wasn't going to learn anything worthwhile, Abby got to her feet. A diagnosis of the little boy's condition would have to wait for Dr. Maclaine.

Abby hated to give up. They saved a lot of time in treatment rooms by having volunteers gather information in the waiting room. So far, all she had written on Bradley's admitting form was a name, address, telephone number, and insurance information.

But the grim, stubborn set of Mrs. Duval's mouth told her it was hopeless.

Then Bradley, his eyes still closed, murmured, "I fell."

Surprised, Abby's eyes shot from the mother to the child. "You fell?" And she thought, *Again?* "That wouldn't give you a stomachache. Where did you fall? What did you hurt?"

The big, brown eyes opened then, looked up at Abby, all innocence and pain. "I fell down the cellar stairs. I'm not supposed to go down there, but my new puppy was down there and he was cryin', and I wanted to tell him not to cry. And I fell. But all I hurt was my arm." He pushed the right sleeve of his blue, cable-knit sweater up to the elbow. A layer of skin had been scraped away from wrist to elbow. The small, lower arm looked like raw meat.

Seeing the look on Abby's face, Mrs. Duval said defensively, "I cleaned it up and disinfected it, and I gave him children's aspirin. The liquid kind. And I don't see what the fall could have to do with his stomachache. I'm sure they're not related."

"Maybe not. But you should have told me he had fallen *again*. Dr. Maclaine will want to know."

"I'll *tell* Dr. Maclaine," the woman said icily. She tugged her son's sweater sleeve back into place. He winced.

Abby winced, too. She didn't believe he'd fallen again. Having five younger siblings had taught her that children were constantly tumbling over and out of and into things. But how often did those falls send them to the hospital? None of her sisters or her brother had ever required emergency care following a fall. They'd scraped themselves off, received the necessary first aid from a parent, with maybe a cookie to soothe the pain, and gone on their merry way.

This was Bradley's *fourth* visit.

"I didn't mean to snap at you," the woman apologized to Abby. Her eyes were very dark, almost black, and Abby saw little contrition in them, in spite of the woman's words. "I'm just upset. I'm sorry. Could you just go see if Dr. Maclaine is ready for us now? Bradley is in so much pain."

Clipboard in hand, Abby turned and went to inform the pediatrician that Bradley Duval was back in E.R. Again.

"So, how's your fireman?" Susannah asked when Kate joined her in treatment room three. Susannah had just finished cleaning up after a sixteen-year-old who had won a pie-eating contest and lived to regret it.

"I keep telling you, he's not *my* fireman!" Kate busied herself helping Susannah tear off the stained paper sheet and replace it with a clean one. "But he's fine," she added with her sly smile. "He says this is one of the craziest weekends we've had since the blast on campus. So, what's been happening here?"

Susannah filled her in on Julie Whittier and Toni. "We should go check, see what's going on with them." As they left the room, she asked, "You and Damon are coming to the picnic tomorrow, right?"

"Not me. Damon is. He's playing waiter for your folks. Personally, I can't see Damon wearing a white jacket and taking orders, but he says it pays well and he needs the extra money. So what else is new? Me, I might just hang out here. They're probably going to need me. A lot of people are off tomorrow."

"Oh, come on, Kate! You're not scheduled to work. Please come."

"Hey, Grant, don't go getting that wounded-deer look on your face, okay? If it was just you and Sam, and maybe O'Connor and Sid, I'd be there. But all those high society friends of your parents will be there. They'll stare at me, and be very, very polite, and ask me if I tap-dance or play basketball."

Susannah hadn't really expected Kate to show up at the picnic. Kate had only been to Linden Hall once, and that was to return a sweater Susannah had forgotten at Emsee. It wasn't that she hadn't been invited. She had, many times. But she always seemed to be busy. Susannah genuinely liked Kate, and since *she* didn't see any differences between them, she didn't understand why Kate insisted on keeping her distance.

Like Will, Susannah thought. Just like Will.

Had Abby heard the thought, she would have said bluntly, "You, too, Susannah. It isn't always Will who's cautious about his feelings. Sometimes you are, too."

True. Too true. Stock market prices were discussed more often in the Grant household than feelings. Susannah wasn't comfortable saying, "I feel . . ." Worse, most of the time, she didn't *know* how she felt. About practically anything. Except working at Emsee. *That*, she loved, no question.

"There are fireworks again tomorrow night," Kate said as they left the cubicle. "If that bash at Linden Hall is over by nine, maybe you guys can join Damon and me on the riverbank, near the bridge. That's the best view."

"No, it's not. The best view in town is from Linden Hall. Why don't *you* and Damon join *us* up there?" Susannah turned in the hallway to face Kate. Her expression was serious. "Please,

Kate? Just this once? Damon will already be there, anyway."

Kate shrugged. "Maybe. If I can."

Susannah was willing to settle for that. It was more than she'd expected to get from Kate.

An orderly in green rushed past them with a gurney bearing a sheet-covered figure. An attractive woman in a yellow suit, her face pale and drawn, hurried along behind it, accompanied by Bobs Swickert, Patsy Keene, and Abby. Abby's expression was grim, too. She didn't say anything as the group passed Kate and Susannah.

"I wonder what that's all about?" Kate mused. "O'Connor looked like she was gearing up for battle."

"I don't know. Wasn't that a little boy on the table?"

"I couldn't tell. I didn't get a good enough look." Kate pointed. "There's Jeremy. Let's see if he found out anything about that girl. Toni? Isn't that her name?"

Jeremy had been told only that the patient was "holding her own." "Whatever *that* means," he grumbled.

"You're not a relative of Toni's," Kate pointed out. "Even if they had information about her condition, they wouldn't give it to you. You'll just have to be patient."

Jeremy snorted in disgust. "How many times in one day do you people use that phrase? 'You'll

91

just have to be patient'? It's either that one or 'We really don't know anything right now' or 'These things take time.' " His face was reddening with anger. "You people aren't *supposed* to be *guessing*! You're supposed to *know*!"

"Hey, chill," Susannah said calmly, putting a hand on Jeremy's arm. "Kate's right. You hardly know Toni. You can't expect to be given information about her condition." But she felt sorry for him. She could see that he was still feeling responsible for Toni's accident, in spite of what Will had said to him. "Want us to go see what we can find out?"

The anger on Jeremy's square, handsome face was instantly replaced by hope. "You can do that?"

Half a dozen people, most of them in shorts and T-shirts except for a blond woman in a red sundress, burst through the front door just then. They were accompanied by a tall, gray-haired man wearing a black suit with a clergyman's collar. A priest or minister, Susannah realized. Two of the people, a boy and a girl, were teenagers in denim cutoffs and white T-shirts. Both were very sunburned. All of the faces looked anxious. The woman in the red sundress held a tissue to her eyes. The group rushed straight to the elevator, pushed a button and, a few minutes later, disappeared inside.

When the hallway was quiet again, Susannah

asked, "Jeremy, why isn't Callie waiting with you?"

"She went upstairs to see her father," Jeremy answered, returning to his chair in the hallway. "She said she wanted to make sure he was still planning on taking her to the picnic at Linden Hall tomorrow. I guess she was afraid he'd changed his mind."

"We'll be right back," Kate told him. "Don't go away."

"I won't."

Unwilling to wait for an elevator and wanting the exercise, they decided to take the stairs to the fourth floor.

Susannah knew the minute they stepped out into the third floor hall that something was wrong. She could hear it in the ominous silence that greeted them as they opened the fire door. This wasn't Intensive Care, which was always quiet. And it was only around nine or so. Visiting hours would be over, but every Internal Medicine patient wouldn't be asleep this early. There should have been conversation, maybe even laughter from the rooms of patients who were almost ready to be discharged. Nurses should have been calling back and forth to one another, water pitchers should have been clinking as ice cubes were spilled into glasses on bedside tray tables.

But there wasn't a sound. And there was no

one in the white-tiled hallway stretching ahead of them. It was empty except for twin, unoccupied wheelchairs, a folded gurney leaning against one wall, and a mop and bucket stationed beside one of the wheelchairs.

"Creepy," Kate breathed, staying where she was just beyond the door. "Where is everybody? What's going on?"

They stood motionless for a minute or two, straining for some familiar sound, or the sight of someone in white or green or gray to emerge from a room.

When that finally happened, it was a young nurse Susannah didn't recognize. Her head was down as she left a room and walked slowly to the station. She didn't notice the two girls standing at the end of the hall. Sinking into a chair behind the desk, she put her head in her hands.

Susannah and Kate began to move toward her.

They were stopped in their tracks by the sound of a harsh, agonized wail that tore into the silence like a knife, then the unmistakable sound of sobbing.

Kate ran lightly ahead of Susannah, to the nurse. "What's going on?"

The young nurse lifted her head. Though she hadn't been crying, her eyes were red-rimmed. "It's the Whittier girl. She just died."

Susannah overheard. Her mouth fell open in shock. She turned slowly toward the room the nurse had just left. People looking stunned and shaken were beginning to emerge. She recognized them as the group she had seen downstairs, entering the elevator. The woman in the red sundress was crying, and having difficulty walking. A tall man in a white knit shirt put an arm around her waist to support her. The two teenagers were white-faced, their eyes wide with disbelief. Every person in the group moved slowly, shakily, as if uncertain of the floor beneath their feet. They were clearly all in shock.

The priest came out last, a purple scapular around his neck. He moved quickly to the family, putting his arms around the tall man and the woman in red, uttering soft words of comfort that Susannah and Kate couldn't hear.

"Dead?" Kate asked the nurse. When she received a solemn nod in return, she whirled to face Susannah. "I thought you said Julie Whittier had 'summer complaint.' Nobody *dies* from summer complaint, Susannah!"

Hearing an accusation in the comments, Susannah took a step backward, saying defensively, "I *know* that, Kate. I . . . I guess that wasn't Julie's problem."

The nurse glanced up then. "No," she told Susannah and Kate quietly, "it wasn't. That's not what killed her."

—⋀⋀⋀—⋀—⋀—⋀—⋀⋀—

Kate moved around the desk to stand beside the nurse. "Run that by us again? If her stomach problem didn't kill her, what did?"

The nurse, whose plastic identification tag read, "Celia Lewis, R.N.," picked up a sheaf of papers and got to her feet. She stepped around Kate to move to a white steel filing cabinet. Pulling open a top drawer, she bent over it. When she finally answered, she kept her voice low. "I didn't say a stomach problem didn't kill her. I said it wasn't summer complaint."

"Then what *was* it?" Susannah pressed. She couldn't shake the feeling of dread that had overtaken her. Something was wrong here, something more than a tragic death.

The nurse turned and put a finger to her lips, her eyes on the grief-stricken group gathered in the hallway. They had been moving forward slowly, clustered together for comfort, and were close enough now to overhear anything said in a normal tone of voice at the nurses' station.

Susannah and Kate fell silent. Kate was wondering if the guy in cutoffs and T-shirt was Julie Whittier's brother, or a boyfriend. His eyes were blank, unseeing. If he wasn't in shock, he was close to it. But then, they all had to be.

A short, rotund man wearing a gray medical coat and thick eyeglasses, emerged from Julie Whittier's room. Susannah had never seen him before. He was much older than most of the doctors at Emsee, but he walked, in spite of his rounded shape, with the same air of arrogance that carried younger doctors through the halls.

"That's Dr. Sumner," Kate whispered. "Dr. Joe Sumner. He's a surgeon. He's been here at Emsee forever. The joke around here is that his first patient was a dinosaur. Some people say he's the reason they're extinct now." Then she amended, "Actually, he used to be a really super surgeon. That's what my mom told me. But rumor around the hospital has it that he's lost his touch and is too stubborn to step down. I wonder if he's the one who did Whittier's appendectomy."

Behind them, Celia Lewis, still at the filing cabinet, answered quietly, "Yeah, he is. And I wouldn't trade places with him now, *or* the hospital administration, for ten million dollars. Which," she added dryly, "might be what it's going to cost this fine facility to make peace with that girl's family."

Susannah drew in her breath. "He made a mistake in surgery? *That's* what killed her?"

The nurse shrugged. "Who knows? Could have been an infection, though. Maybe from a foreign instrument in her abdomen somewhere?"

The group was still standing in the middle of the hall. They were talking among themselves. Their voices rose as the doctor joined them.

Kate gave Nurse Lewis a long, level look. "You don't know that," she said flatly. "You couldn't, not yet."

Another shrug. "You're right. I'm just a lowly nurse." She turned back to her filing cabinet. Over her shoulder, she added, "I guess we'll just have to wait for the official postmortem to learn the truth. But like they say, truth is relative, right? One person's truth could be another person's cover-up."

Irritated, Susannah turned on the nurse, speaking to her white-uniformed back. "If you think the hospital administration is unethical enough to lie when a doctor screws up or does sloppy work, why do you even work here?" As angry as she was, she was acutely conscious of the group in the hallway not far from where she stood, and kept her voice down.

"Oh, honey, grow up! You just listen to that silver-tongued surgeon down there, hear what he has to say to those people. Then tell me you honestly believe that anyone in this entire medical complex is going to fess up to why that girl *really* died."

Susannah listened. The third floor was still so quiet, as if everyone sensed that a tragedy had taken place, she was able to hear most of what the elderly surgeon said to Julie Whittier's friends and relatives.

"No logical explanation . . . these things happen . . . do a postmortem, of course . . . must have been run-down . . . awfully thin . . . had an eating disorder, did she? . . . that would do it, of course. Does terrible things to the system, you know."

Susannah swallowed hard. Julie Whittier hadn't looked anorexic. Slender, yes, but not unhealthy. Was Dr. Sumner lying? Or was he just mistaken?

A cry of denial rang out in the corridor. It came from the woman in the red sundress. "How *dare* you? My daughter did not suffer from an eating disorder! She was thin because she was an athlete, a runner. But she was healthy! Julie had never been sick a day in her life until appendicitis struck her."

Dr. Sumner's gravelly voice continued unperturbed. "Yes, well, sometimes the parents are the last to know. At any rate, rest assured that we will discover the cause of this unfortunate episode."

The tall man in the knit shirt exploded. "Episode? *Episode?* Our fifteen-year-old daughter, who was perfectly healthy until last month, is dead and you call it an episode? Something is very wrong here, Doctor, and believe me when I tell you that I intend to find out exactly what that something is. I won't rest until I know what took our daughter from us. And for your information, she hadn't been feeling up to par since she came home following the surgery that *you* performed!"

Then the tears began again and everyone stopped talking.

Dr. Sumner adjusted the stethoscope around his neck, raised the clipboard in his hand as if it might shield him from their emotion, and said stiffly, "I understand that you're upset. But you wouldn't want to say anything that you might regret later. I'll get back to you when the post-mortem has given us our answers. You will, of course, want an autopsy."

Mrs. Whittier began to cry again. "No, no, Jack, don't let them do that to her!"

Her husband bent his head toward hers. "We need to know, Marta. You want to know *why*, don't you?" When she didn't answer, he gave the doctor a reluctant nod.

Dr. Sumner turned and walked away, disappearing into an elevator.

He didn't walk like someone overwhelmed with either guilt *or* grief, Susannah thought.

The priest was attempting to console the family as they, too, filed into an elevator. He wasn't having much luck with the white-shirted man who kept repeating, "This isn't the end of this, not the end of this by a long shot."

When the elevator doors had closed, Kate said to Susannah, "We'd better get back downstairs. We've been gone too long."

Susannah nodded. But she stayed where she was. "Nurse Lewis, they brought a girl up here from Emergency a while ago. Her name is Toni, she's about our age. She had a stomach problem, too, and she'd taken a bad fall. How is she?"

Without turning away from the file cabinet, the nurse answered, "The Barnes girl? She's not here."

Relief swept over Susannah. "She's been discharged already?"

"I didn't say that. I said she isn't here. They took her up to ICU half an hour ago."

"She's in Intensive Care?" Susannah was stunned. "But . . . but she wasn't that sick! Did she break something in that fall? She didn't fracture her skull, did she?"

The nurse turned around then, returned to her desk. "I don't know anything about any fall. No broken bones, though. And no head injury. She was transferred to ICU because her blood pressure was skyrocketing and she was wracked by diarrhea and nausea. A hint of jaundice, too. Lobell wanted round-the-clock supervision for her, so off to ICU she went. Lobell was mad because we couldn't reach her parents. He needed some forms signed." She looked at Susannah. "You don't happen to know where her folks might be, do you? We've tried calling them at home. No one answers."

"No. But her date is downstairs. He might know. I'll check."

"Her symptoms weren't identical to Whittier's, were they?" Kate asked.

The nurse looked surprised. "Identical? No. Why would they be? There were some similarities, I guess, but the Barnes girl came in because of a fall, and the Whittier girl had surgery a month ago. Not much similarity there, I'd say."

Although Kate and Susannah discussed the two cases during the elevator ride downstairs, neither knew what to think. Both cases were unsettling. And now Julie Whittier was dead.

Greta Schwinn had already heard, and was visibly upset. "That poor child. She really didn't seem that ill when she was admitted." She assigned Susannah to the waiting room, saying it was "overflowing," and asked Kate to help with the young Duval boy. "There's something really fishy about *that* whole business," she said grimly. "The only five-year-olds who come in here that often are kids suffering from chronic diseases. Bradley Duval doesn't *have* a chronic disease. Repeated falling is *not* a disease, especially in a young child."

"It could be a symptom of something chronic, though," Kate suggested, then added, "But I guess he's already been tested for something like that, right?"

Nurse Schwinn didn't know.

"I could check his records," Kate offered. "See what tests he's geen given."

"Dr. Maclaine has his records. They're in treatment room three. And Thompson," the head nurse added, "let the doctor do the detective work, okay? She's equipped for it. We're not."

"Yeah, sure." Kate grinned at Susannah, and headed for the cubicle.

Susannah was on her way to the waiting room when a tall, thin, striking-looking woman in snug black leather jeans and a sleeveless red crop top, black spike heels on her feet, clickety-clacked her way through the lobby toward Susannah. When she got close enough, Susannah recognized Letitia Simone. She walked with a sense of purpose, and broke into a smile when she spotted Susannah.

"Hi, Susie-Q, how's it goin'? Have you seen Jer?" A three-strand gold necklace glittered under the overhead fluorescent fixtures. Matching earrings dangled like liquid gold.

"Hi, Tish. How are the picnic plans coming along? Mom finally set you free?" Susannah was always glad to see Tish, but there wasn't time to talk to her now. What was she doing here? Why was she looking for Jeremy?

Tish waved a thin, bronzed arm dismissively. "Everything's all set for tomorrow. Is Jeremy here? I went to the house to return something his father had left at my condo, but no one was there. A neighbor said someone got sick at the party and an ambulance had to be called. Has something happened to Jeremy?"

"No. It was his date. A girl named Toni Barnes." A sudden thought occurred to Susannah. Although Tish herself wasn't wealthy, many of her friends were. Like the Barnes family. If Tish knew where Toni's parents were tonight, Susannah could take that information upstairs. Then Jeremy wouldn't have to make the painful telephone call himself. The nurse on four would do it. "You don't by any chance know Toni's parents, do you?"

Tish, swinging her car keys absentmindedly as her eyes behind the red-framed glasses surveyed the lobby, nodded. "Sure. I know Artie and Liz." She rolled her eyes. "Bor-ing! Like most truly dull people, they don't *know* they're dull. So they throw a lot of parties, which, in spite of my best efforts, are always about as much fun as heat rash. But they're loaded, so I never turn down the work." Her eyes returned to Susannah. "Their kid is sick?"

Two ambulances wailed to a stop at the back entrance at the same time. Susannah asked impatiently, "Do you *know* where her parents can be reached, Tish? They're not home."

"Nope. Haven't a clue," Tish said airily. Spying Jeremy sitting in a dim corner of the lobby, she said, "There he is!" and would have moved toward him if she hadn't realized instantly that he wasn't alone. A nurse was sitting with him, talking to him quietly.

Noticing who Tish was looking at, Susannah said, "That's Patsy Keene. She works here."

"I *know* who Patsy *Keene* is, Susannah." The bitterness was back. "And now that I know he's okay, I'll just toddle along. Tell him I was asking about him, okay? Or not. What*ever*. See you tomorrow." Her steps as she clickety-clacked back to the door and pushed it open were no longer purposeful. They sounded, instead, angry.

Susannah didn't blame her. Patsy Keene had been Tish's replacement with Dr. Barlow. Of course, that hadn't lasted, either, which must have given Tish *some* comfort. But probably not nearly enough.

Jeremy had actually liked Patsy, at least a little, and had been disappointed when his father moved on to what Jeremy cynically called "the next one." Hadn't that been Bobs Swickert? As nice as Bobs was, by that time Jeremy had decided not to become friendly with any of his father's dates. It seemed clear that none of them would become permanent fixtures in his life.

Never mind that. What she had to do now was go tell Jeremy that Toni Barnes was a lot sicker than they'd thought. Jeremy was one of those people who *seemed* to take bad news fairly well. He wouldn't faint, or cry out, or fly into a rage at the unfairness of it all, the way some people did. But he would be every bit as miserable as someone who *did* do all of those things. And in this case, Susannah was afraid, he would probably blame himself. She would have to make it very clear that Toni's trip to ICU was not connected to the fall she'd taken at Jeremy's party.

Taking a deep breath and letting it out, Susannah hurried across the lobby toward Jeremy.

chapter
12

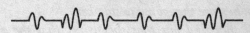

I don't get it. How did a child become involved?

This is not good.

I know that woman. She's brought her kid into the E.R. more than once. There have been rumors about her for a long time now. But no one ever followed up on them. They said it was because there wasn't any proof, and the child always told the examining physician that he'd had an accident.

Sure. And I'm getting married tomorrow to the man of my dreams.

They're lying about why nothing was done in the Duval case. It's really because that woman's husband and her father are Very Important People in Grant. Samuel Grant himself is a close friend of theirs.

I did not touch a bottle of children's aspirin! I would never do something like that. That would make me a monster. I'm not a monster. And it isn't children I'm angry with, never children.

That terrible mother! She's lying. She couldn't have given him children's aspirin, not if he's been poisoned. Even if it was accidental . . . because she couldn't, of course, have known . . . it's still her fault. Why did she have to give him medication in the first place? Because she'd hurt him, that's why. That much I'm sure of. Just like she did those other times. So it's her fault.

When are they going to stop her?

If they find out that she's lying, that she never gave him children's aspirin at all, they'll do more digging. They might actually find something, if they dig hard enough. I don't want them to, not yet. Only when I'm ready. Then I'll tell it, all of it.

But not yet. It isn't time. Things have to go according to my plan. And they would have, if it weren't for that stupid woman. They still could. I don't think anyone will dig too hard, because of who that family is. I still have time.

I didn't hurt that child. That's one thing I'm going to make clear.

When the time comes.

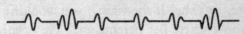

On her way to Jeremy, Susannah passed the waiting room. The crowd had thinned a little. Susannah knew that wasn't necessarily a good sign. On weekend nights, especially on holiday weekends, it might mean only that from now on, the injuries would be more serious, with patients entering by ambulance at the back door rather than walking in through the front entrance to take a seat in the waiting room.

Jeremy was still sitting in a chair in the lobby, still wearing his jacket and tie. He was leaning back, his head against the wall, his eyes closed. Patsy was sitting silently beside him, holding one of his hands.

When Susannah reached them, she put a hand on Jeremy's shoulder.

He opened his eyes and jerked upright, senses alert. When he saw Susannah, he asked, "How is she? Is Toni okay? Can I take her home now?"

With a smile and a wave, Patsy got up quietly and left, leaving Jeremy to Susannah.

Taking a seat beside him, she said, "Jeremy, do

you happen to know where Toni's parents might be?"

In answer, he groaned. His head fell back against the wall, and his eyes closed again. "I knew it!" he cried softly, "I just knew it! She's worse, isn't she? If she wasn't, you wouldn't want to know where her parents are." He opened his eyes, looked directly into Susannah's. "Is Toni going to die?"

In treatment room three, the attractive woman in the yellow suit was explaining exactly how her five-year-old son had arrived at the hospital on this fourth occasion. "Of course I ran down the cellar stairs the very second I heard him fall," she told Dr. Maclaine. Patsy and Bobs were working on Bradley, and Kate was holding one of his hands. Abby was waiting impatiently in the outside hall. "I thought he was in the living room watching cartoons, and suddenly I heard this thunk, thunk, thunk noise in the cellar doorway, like a basketball bouncing down the steps. But Bradley doesn't *have* a basketball. I knew what it was immediately, and I can tell you, Doctor, my heart jumped right into my throat."

Patsy and Bobs exchanged a skeptical glance, but continued silently with their work. Patsy was wrapping a blood-pressure cuff around the boy's upper arm, while Bobs took his temperature.

"I checked him over carefully," Beth Duval continued. "I made sure that he wasn't seriously hurt. There was just that little scrape on his arm."

Little? Kate stared at the raw-hamburger look of the boy's arm. Mother of the Year, she thought sarcastically, then wondered why she was so angry with Mrs. Duval. In spite of the rumors, which they had all heard, there was no real evidence that this woman was anything less than a wonderfully nurturing parent. Didn't she bring him to the hospital each time he was injured? Didn't that make her a good mother?

That depended on how he'd been injured in the first place.

"I treated the scrape, gave him some aspirin . . . children's aspirin, of course . . . and rocked him for a while until he stopped crying. He seemed fine for a while."

"Did his stomach strike something in the basement when he landed?" Dr. Maclaine asked, checking the boy's ears.

"I don't think so." Mrs. Duval was clutching one of Bradley's hands in both of hers. He had been lying still during the examination, but now he cried out and began writhing in pain on the table. "I didn't notice anything at the foot of the stairs. But then, I was concentrating on Bradley."

Patsy, looking skeptical, was struggling to take blood from the agitated child. Bobs had taken his temperature, announcing, "Ninety-eight point six" when she finished.

"No fever. Good, very good. No infection. What then?" Dr. Maclaine mused aloud. "So," she asked the mother, "he's only been like this for ... what? A few hours? All evening? How long?"

"It started around four o'clock, I guess. I was making potato salad for our picnic supper. We were going to eat out on the patio. Such a lovely night . . ."

Dr. Maclaine glanced at her watch. "Four o'clock? It's ten-thirty. What took you so long to get him here?"

The woman's flush deepened, this time with resentment. "My husband says I'm overprotective, that I drag Bradley over here too often. I thought I could handle it myself. I gave him more children's aspirin and put him to bed. But then he started throwing up . . ."

Bobs had removed the little boy's sandals. "Why are his feet swollen?" Dr. Maclaine asked suddenly.

Kate peered, and could see that the small feet were indeed swollen. Except for the pinkish color, they looked like pears.

Mrs. Duval shook her head. "He must have hurt them when he fell."

There was, then, a prolonged, uncertain silence during which Dr. Maclaine moved to the side of the table to remove Bradley's hand from his mother's and turn it over and over in her own competent hands. Kate thought the small hands looked swollen, too, though not as severely as his feet. Then the doctor examined the patient's eyes for a second time.

Bradley began crying, softly, his sobs clearly anguished. He turned on his side, drawing his knees up into his chest, his hands clawing at his stomach. Patsy tried to comfort him, but it didn't help.

When Dr. Maclaine finally stepped away from the table, her eyes remaining on the small, tortured figure, she said slowly, thoughtfully, "I think a toxicology scan might be in order. And," she added more firmly, "I would like the results *yesterday*."

One of the nurses, blood samples in hand, rushed from the room.

"Toxicology?" Mrs. Duval asked, her voice quavering. "Why do you need that?"

"I need that," Dr. Maclaine answered, her own voice unemotional and perfectly level, "to confirm or refute my theory that your son has been poisoned."

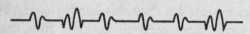

The word "poisoned" bounced around the treatment room like a rubber ball, slamming into first one pair of ears, then another and another until everyone in the room except Dr. Maclaine was openmouthed with disbelief.

Including Mrs. Duval. When she found her voice, she whispered, "Poison? What are you *talking* about?"

"Take this child upstairs to Pediatrics ICU," the doctor ordered Patsy, who had been daubing the little boy's injured arm with antiseptic-soaked cotton. "I'm going to the lab to follow up on those tests. Mrs. Duval, you'll be staying with your boy?" Without waiting for an answer, she stripped off her rubber gloves, handed them to Bobs, nodded curtly in the direction of the stricken mother, turned and left the room.

"Poisoned?" Mrs. Duval whispered again. The sound echoed hollowly in the sudden silence that followed Dr. Maclaine's departure. "No, no, that's impossible. He's just . . . he's just sick!"

Mrs. Duval went upstairs with her son. Patsy

sent an orderly with them. When they had gone, the nurses clucked their tongues in disapproval. Patsy added, "If there's one thing I just can't stand, it's cowards who pick on little kids! It's disgusting, obscene . . ."

Bobs nodded agreement, but added, "This time, maybe we'll get somewhere! That woman isn't going to be able to worm her way out of this one, not if Dr. Maclaine has anything to say about it."

Kate left to tell Abby, impatiently bouncing up and down on her sneakers in the hall, what had taken place inside and why Bradley and his mother had gone upstairs.

She had a feeling Abby wouldn't be that shocked.

"I don't *know* where Toni lives," Jeremy confessed to Susannah when she asked. "Somewhere on the west side, that's all I know. I told you, I just met the girl on Tuesday. But her number must be in the phone book."

"It is. No one answers. Her parents must be out. We'll just have to wait until they get home, I guess." Susannah thought for a minute. An ambulance siren died at the back door, then another followed. She couldn't sit here all night with Jeremy. "How about if you keep calling her house until someone answers? It'll give you something to do."

Jeremy shook his head. "I don't know what to say to her parents. I've never met them. I didn't pick her up at her house tonight, she came on her own. She got a ride with a friend who was on his way to the band concert downtown. He dropped her off and left. I guess she was planning on me taking her home. And I would have," Jeremy's head drooped, "if she hadn't ended up *here*."

"Just keep trying to reach her parents, okay, Jer? And don't worry. Toni will probably be fine." She deliberately used the word "probably." If there was one thing Susannah couldn't stand, it was doctors and nurses who told relatives and friends of a patient, "I'm sure he/she will be fine" when there was *no* reason to believe that was true. It wasn't fair, and Susannah thought it was stupid. It just made the shock worse when the patient didn't recover.

Jeremy didn't look all that well himself. His face was paler than usual, his eyes bleak. But he promised to do his best to locate Toni's parents.

When she had that promise, Susannah ran to the back entrance to see if she could be of any help.

The patients from the first ambulance had already been dispatched to trauma rooms. The second load was just being removed on stretchers. Dr. Izbecki, Patsy Keene, Bobs, and two orderlies were waiting just beyond the vehicle's open rear doors. A third ambulance arrived, squealing up the driveway and screeching to a halt behind the other two.

"Let's move it, people!" Dr. Izbecki called out.

The open ambulance yielded two victims of a car wreck. One had suffered a broken clavicle, fractured left arm, a deep laceration on the left knee, and shallower lacerations about the face and neck. He was about twenty years old, conscious, and calling for his mother. The second victim was awake and very agitated. When he was placed on a gurney, he tried desperately to throw himself off, and had to be restrained with straps. He had no visible outer injuries beyond a swollen right cheekbone, but his blood pressure was reported by the paramedics as being so low, internal injuries were probable.

The smell of liquor permeated both victims.

Idiots! Susannah thought. But that didn't stop her from running alongside the gurneys without waiting to see what the third ambulance had brought them. She didn't learn until much later that its contents included another victim of stomach distress. He had collapsed in pain at the wheel of his car and slammed into a stone support of the Hickory Street bridge, fracturing his skull and both legs. Susannah recognized the man. His name was Curtis Brandywine. He suffered from chronic arthritis and often showed up in the E.R. needing pain relief.

This time, he spent no more than a few minutes in a trauma room before being dispatched upstairs to surgery.

By the time the two accident victims had been treated and transferred out of Emergency, waiting-room occupants were beginning to spill over into the hall. In the E.R. itself, every cubicle was filled.

"Now the *real* fun begins," Greta Schwinn said when Susannah returned to the station for a new assignment. "You don't have to stay, you know. You're not officially on duty."

"I'm staying. Where do you want me?"

Nurse Schwinn looked down at the clipboard in her hands. "Well, let's see . . . You've seen the mess in the waiting room. O'Connor's been a big help, taking info and calming people down. She talked Dr. Barlow's kid into helping her. Finally got him off the phone. I think he was looking for someone. Must have found them, because he started lending a hand here."

Jeremy had located the Barnes parents. Good. Susannah wondered how they'd taken the news that a simple earache had developed into a serious condition that had sent their daughter to ICU.

"Now about the rooms . . . there's a second-degree burn in four that needs saline and a dressing before discharge, and a drunk in five who tripped over his own dog when he tottered home, fell and broke his wrist." Nurse Schwinn chuckled. "The guy's wrist, not the dog's." Then she went blithely on, "Room two is a woman who wanted a better look at the fireworks so she went out on a cliff above the river, and fell about two stories. X ray has people stacked up and she's had to wait, so we've got her on strict spine stabilization precautions, just in case. You might want to go in and clean her up a bit, talk to her, keep her calm. You know, the kind of thing you're aces at."

The compliment went unnoticed. Susannah was concentrating on the fact that Nurse Schwinn had not mentioned another "stomach distress" case like Julie and Toni. That was something, anyway. Although in view of what was going on, it seemed a small blessing. Before she headed for room two, she poked her head into the waiting room to call out to Abby.

"Did you hear?" Abby asked breathlessly when she arrived at Susannah's side. Jeremy was still inside, taking information from an angry-looking man holding a bloody towel over his left hand. "About the poison?"

"Poison? *What* poison?"

Abby shared Dr. Maclaine's theory about Bradley Duval in rapid-fire sentences. Susannah stood perfectly still, not interrupting once. All of her energy went toward digesting what Abby was saying.

When Abby ran out of breath and words, Susannah was silent for a second or two. Then, "It makes sense, doesn't it?"

Abby stared at her. "What does?"

"She said he fell down the stairs. But she also said his stomach didn't strike anything when he landed. So why would he come here with a stomachache? Maybe poison makes sense." Susannah spoke more calmly than she actually felt. The thought of a mother poisoning her own child was sickening, repulsive. But feelings weren't thoughts, and in spite of what she was feeling, her mind was working logically to find the answer to a puzzle. That was just the way she was. "It could be an accidental poisoning. Dr. Maclaine didn't actually accuse Mrs. Duval, did she? Little kids get into things they shouldn't all the time . . . medicines, drain cleaners, insecticides, gasoline. We've seen it more than once in E.R."

"And if Mrs. Duval didn't have any *history* here," Abby said bitterly, "that's probably what everyone *would* be thinking. That Bradley had accidentally swallowed something he shouldn't have. But they've been in here too many times. If people suspect her, it's her own fault. I *still* think she's been abusing him, and I'm not the only one."

The subject was too bizarre to discuss when there was so much else to do. "We'll talk about it later, okay? Listen, Abby, did Jeremy get in touch with Toni's parents?"

"Yeah, he did. I think they're already upstairs."

"How'd they take the news?"

"I don't know. I haven't seen them. All Jeremy said was that he'd found them and they were coming right over. That was about twenty minutes ago. Jeremy looks almost as bad as Toni must feel. And they won't let him see her because he's not family. I feel sorry for him."

"Grant!" Greta Schwinn's voice called. "Where *are* you? That woman in two is getting restless. She *has* to lie perfectly still. Go in and sing to her or something."

"Later," Abby told Susannah, and went back into the waiting room to help Jeremy calm the man holding the bloody towel.

When the young woman who had fallen off the cliff had been wheeled upstairs for X rays, Susannah took a moment to call Will and tell him about the suspicions running rampant in the hospital. First, she told him about Julie Whittier.

He wasn't that surprised. "Rumors about Dr. Joe Sumner's shaky hands and failing memory have been circulating like stale air ever since I started at Med Center. Patsy Keene told me they insisted that he step down, maybe take a chair at

121

the University, but he refused. Said he's going to operate until they have to carry him out of the operating room. Some surgeons are like that. It's all they care about . . . operating. You take that away from them and they don't know what to do."

Then Susannah told him about Bradley Duval.

That *did* surprise Will. He was speechless for a moment or two. "Poisoned? By his own mother?"

"No one knows that yet, Will," Susannah said quickly. Spreading accusations against a possibly innocent woman could create enormous legal problems for the hospital. She would have to be more careful. Still, this was *Will.* She couldn't *not* tell him. "They don't know for sure that it *is* poison. The tests aren't back yet. And even if it *is* poison, it could have been accidental. He's only five. He could have ingested something when his mother wasn't looking."

"I was on duty for two of the Duval emergency calls," Will said. "That house was immaculate. It looked like something out of a magazine. And Mrs. Duval asked us to scrape our shoes off on the mat on the front porch so we wouldn't bring dirt inside. Everything in that house was in its proper place. She didn't strike me as the type of mother who would carelessly leave poisonous substances around for her kid to get his hands on."

And, Susannah thought, I'll bet she didn't strike you as the type who would physically abuse her child, either. But a lot of people at Emsee are convinced that she did.

"I can't believe you're still over there," Will said then. "You've got a big day ahead of you tomorrow. You should get some sleep."

"I'll leave the second it calms down. It's been awful here. I wish you were on duty. How are you feeling, anyway?" Susannah thought of Julie Whittier, and of Toni Barnes. What if Will had the same thing they did?

"Great. I ate a huge dinner. No problem. So, I guess I'll see you tomorrow? Two o'clock?"

"Yep." Susannah smiled into the telephone. "You're not going to chicken out on me at the last minute, are you? You *are* ready for this, right?"

"I was born ready." But in the next minute, Will added, "Of course, I could have a relapse. Then I'd have to beg off."

"Will! That's not funny! You just said you were perfectly fine."

"Relax, will you? I was kidding. I'll be there."

Uneasy, Susannah said, "I'm working for a few hours in the morning, so call me here, first thing, and tell me you're okay. Please?"

"What if I'm not? Should I lie?"

"Yes. Lie. And show up at Linden Hall at two."

Greta Schwinn's voice rang out, "Grant! We've got an eight-year-old tossing his cookies in room two! Get over here! And bring a bucket!"

Susannah didn't even take the time to tell Will good-bye. She knew he would understand.

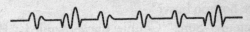

It was after three-thirty in the morning when things had calmed down enough for Susannah and Abby to leave Med Center. Although Jeremy looked exhausted, he refused to go with them. Susannah hated to leave Jeremy, but at least Toni's parents were with him now. She took a moment on her way out of the hospital to ask one of the ICU nurses about Toni.

"She's hangin' in there." The nurse, Connie Brewer, had worked in E.R. a few times, and was a favorite of Susannah's. She was pretty and friendly, and as good a diagnostician as some doctors. "Her parents are here now, so if she requires any extraordinary procedures, we can get their permission."

The news could have been worse, but still, the phrase "extraordinary procedures" was depressing. Connie Brewer was talking about a girl who had, only hours earlier, been sliding down a stair railing at Jeremy Barlow's house. Until her fall, nothing about her had suggested serious illness.

"Would you do me a favor?" Susannah asked

quietly. "My friend, Jeremy Barlow . . . he's in the waiting room. It was his party tonight. That's where Toni got sick. He's feeling really bad, and he's worried about her. Could you check on him every once in a while, make sure he's okay? If you're not too busy?"

"Jeremy? Sure." Connie Brewer smiled. "He's an okay kid. I kind of feel sorry for him, his mother taking off that way, and Dr. Barlow so busy over here. He must spend a lot of time alone." She was one of the few nurses at Emsee who hadn't dated Dr. Barlow. She was already happily married. "I'll try to see that Jeremy's comfortable while he's up here. Don't worry about him."

Susannah had barely stepped inside her bedroom when the exhaustion hit her. She collapsed on the canopied bed in her clothes, and was asleep in minutes.

Callie had been careful not to drive too closely behind Sam's silver van as he traveled to Rehab, parked, helped Sid into the building, and then drove on to Abby's house, where Lily was renting the O'Connors' garage apartment. When Sam and Lily had gone inside, Callie drove her own small robin's-egg-blue sportscar around the corner where she wouldn't be seen by anyone going into or coming out of the apartment, but from where she had a perfect view, through the treetops, of Lily's windows. The curtains were lace, so Callie had no problem making out the shadowy figures behind them. One was tall, and broad-shouldered . . . Sam. The other . . . the one who turned to him with her face tilted upward when they got inside . . . was tall, too, but thinner, and decidedly feminine. Lily.

Damn her! Callie thought vehemently, rolling down her window to get a better view. A balmy breeze teased her face, as if to say, Don't you wish that you were up there with Sam?

Of course she did. And if Lily Dolan hadn't come along a few months earlier, Sam-and-Callie *would* have happened, Callie was sure of it. He'd already dated almost every girl in town, and none of those romances had lasted. That, Callie had repeatedly told herself, was because he knew as well as she did that the two of them belonged together, so why develop a relationship with some other girl?

Her mother said she was an impatient girl. Her mother was wrong. Callie had been waiting a long time for Sam. They had dated, occasionally, and not once on any of those dates had she pressured him, begged him to stop seeing other girls because she knew they were destined to be together. She'd been willing to wait, even though there were a zillion high school parties and dances she'd had to go to with other boys because Sam was going with someone else. She'd been willing to wait because she knew absolutely that, sooner or later, Sam would settle down with *her*.

But for now, there they were, Sam and Lily, behind the lace curtains in a garage apartment. They were together on a warm May night with air so soft and gentle no one should have been breathing it in lonely solitude. It looked very much as if they were dancing. Dancing!

Callie leaned her head out the window and strained to hear. Yes, there it was, slow, seductive music, as sweet as the night air. And it was coming from up *there*, just as she had known it would be.

Callie pulled her head back inside and leaned against the back of the seat. Tears slid down her cheeks. She watched as the two shadowy figures in pale yellow light behind white lace moved around the room, staying so close together they seemed to be one figure.

The two heads in shadow moved closer together, their lips met . . .

In the warm, sweet, darkness, alone in her car, Callie saw that kiss. The headache that had begun at the base of her neck crawled up her skull and intensified. She felt a scream of pain welling up inside of her.

With great effort, Callie reached into the glove box and pulled out a small, plastic bottle with a

Grant Pharmaceuticals red-and-white label on the side. With shaking hands, she struggled with the childproof cap until it snapped off. She yanked free the thick wad of cotton, tipped the bottle upside down until two white capsules dropped into her palm.

Because she had nothing to drink, she had to swallow them dry.

Then, with one last red-hot glance of rage toward the pale yellow light coming from the apartment and the two heads still so close together, Callie went home.

chapter
16

When Susannah awoke on Sunday morning and went to an open window to take a healthy gulp of fresh air, she found herself looking down upon a tropical paradise. Although it wasn't yet ten o'clock, the hilltop was thriving with activity.

The giant baskets of flowers seemed to be everywhere, dotted across the broad expanse of green as if randomly placed, though Susannah knew that her mother and Tish had chosen the spots only after a great deal of thought and planning. Vines bearing bright red blossoms as large as saucers trailed up the sides and over the top of the white gazebo. Workmen in shorts and T-shirts were cleaning the pool and hot tub, sweeping the cement walkways and hurrying in and out of the cabana carrying piles of thick, white towels, or coolers filled with cold drinks to stock the small refrigerator inside. Tish, wearing a short print dress that swung around her tanned legs as she worked, was directing two of her assistants. They were busy covering the large, round tables with pristine white cloths that fell to the ground. Susannah sat down on the windowseat to watch as fat glass bowls filled with pink and blue hydrangea blossoms were placed at the center of every table.

At the far end of the lawn, a group of men headed by Susannah's father were setting up the fireworks display scheduled for that evening.

You'd think we were having a wedding instead of a picnic, she thought, smiling. The smile disappeared as she wondered if Tish was thinking the same thing. Was part of the reason for Tish's bad mood this past week a wish that all of her preparations were for something far more exciting than a Memorial Day picnic? Susannah knew Letitia wanted to get married. Tish was honest about it. "I want a kid like you someday," she had confided in Susannah shortly after they first met, "and my old biological clock is ticking. Your mom's way ahead of me in that department."

"You're a lot younger than Mom," Susannah had said helpfully.

"Maybe. But you don't see a line of prospective husbands trailing along behind me, begging for my hand in marriage, do you, Susie-Q? I don't believe in putting the cart before the horse, so the husband has to come before the kid."

But no more than a week later, Tish had started dating Dr. Barlow, and Susannah had been delighted. Even when Jeremy complained that Tish wasn't *anything* like his mother, which was true, Susannah's hopes had remained high. She didn't think that Dr. Barlow would be *looking* for a clone of his former wife. After all, look what had happened to *that* relationship.

Then, a month ago, she and Abby, Will and Sid, had stopped in a local restaurant for something to eat after a movie, and there had been Dr. Barlow, sitting at a table holding, not Tish Simone's hand, but Patsy Keene's. The petite blond nurse was gazing at him with adoration in her big, blue eyes.

Susannah had been devastated for Tish. She had been so happy, walking around in a kind of glow. Susannah could almost hear the wedding bells ringing in Tish's head.

But the next time she saw her, the glow was gone, in its place shadows under the eyes, a tightening of the lips, and a new slump to the thin shoulders.

Patsy Keene had certainly seemed happy enough. For a while. A very short while. Then Roberta Swickert had taken Patsy's place. Then Greta Schwinn, and then . . . Susannah, thoroughly disgusted, had stopped keeping track.

She was glad Dr. Barlow was out of town and wouldn't be attending the picnic. Easier for Tish that way. And for Patsy, and Greta, and Bobs . . .

"Men!" she cried out in disgust, as she walked into her bathroom and swept a thick white towel off the rack.

She was just about to step into the shower when her phone rang. She would have let the machine take it if she hadn't thought it might be Will. She wanted to make sure he was feeling okay this morning.

"Susannah?" a quavering voice inquired when she said hello. "It's Callie. Susannah, I'm sick. I am really sick."

Susannah's first reaction was, This is just another trick. Callie's up to something, as always, feigning sickness in order to get attention. She's probably still angry because Sam was with Lily last night.

"Oh, cut it out, Callie," Susannah said in disgust. "I'm busy. Whatever it is you want, I don't have time for it."

"No, Susannah, wait, don't hang up." Callie's voice sounded weird. The normally loud, nasal whine had become a weak, plaintive cry.

Callie *had* played a major role in the junior class play. And she hadn't been half bad in the part of a nasty stepsister. Everyone at school had said it was simply type-casting, not much of an acting challenge for Callie. Was she acting now?

"I really feel horrible, Susannah. I don't know what's wrong. I'm *never* sick. I figured, since you volunteer at Emsee, maybe you could tell me what to do."

Adjusting the oversized towel wrapped around her, Susannah sank down on the rose-colored velvet chaise lounge, her bare feet crossed on the thick carpet. "Callie, your father is the administrator at Emsee. Okay, so he's not a doctor, but I don't think he'd have any trouble *finding* one for you. So why are you calling *me*?"

"I don't *want* a doctor! If I tell my father I'm sick, he'll drag me over to Emsee and then I'll miss out on the picnic this afternoon. That's *not* going to happen, Susannah. Just tell me what to take, and I'll take it, okay?"

The early-morning sun streamed in through the windows and curled around Susannah's toes. It was going to be a beautiful day for a picnic. Susannah smiled. Of course. Her mother had seen to that. "Callie, I won't have my M. D. for years. I can't prescribe medicine. And if you're feeling half as sick as you sound, you *should* go over to Emsee. Have Izbecki check you out. If it isn't anything serious, he'll give you something, like he gave Will, and maybe you can still come to the picnic."

Then Callie sounded more like herself as she shouted into the telephone, "Oh, forget it! I should have known better than to call you! You don't want me at the picnic! I'll figure out what to take myself. Thanks, Susannah, thanks a heap!" Click.

Well, I *did* tell her to go to Emsee, Susannah told herself defensively as she went into the bathroom. If she doesn't go, that's her choice. I'm not her mother.

Half an hour later, while Susannah was drying her hair, Abby called to say the test results on Bradley Duval hadn't come back yet. "He's better this morning, though, according to Astrid. I just called there. She said she'll be coming to the picnic around three, when she gets off duty, and she might know something by then. I hope so. Maybe then they'll finally do something about his mother." The word "mother" was loaded with contempt.

Susannah knew it was pointless to remind Abby that Mrs. Duval's guilt was still in question. Abby had already made up her mind. She asked, instead, about Toni.

"All Connie would tell me is that Toni is holding her own. I guess that means she's not worse, right? So that's good."

Susannah decided to tell Abby about Callie's phone call.

"So, what's your best guess?" Abby asked when Susannah had finished. "We got lucky and she really *is* sick? Which means we won't have to put up with her this afternoon? Which means it'll be a great Memorial Day picnic? Or was she faking?"

"Beats me." Susannah was silent for a moment, then added, "I guess I wasn't thinking about Julie and Toni when Callie called. Maybe she really *is* sick. With the same thing."

"You're hinting that it's contagious, Susannah. Bobs said it wasn't, didn't she?"

135

"Bobs isn't a doctor. And I didn't mean that it was contagious. Maybe they just all ate the same thing, somewhere, like in the same restaurant. It could be anything, really. And could be anywhere. In a fast-food place, in someone's cupboard or refrigerator, or, worse, on a store shelf, just waiting to be taken home and swallowed."

"Susannah!" Abby wailed. "You are ruining my day! How can I have any fun at a picnic when you talk like this? A picnic means *food*. And you're talking about *poisoned* food, with some nasty bacteria or virus or something hidden among its crumbs, something we can't even see or smell. Cut it out, okay?"

"Sorry. You're right. Anyway, Callie was probably doing one of her Academy Award numbers on me. Forget it." They talked about the picnic for a few minutes, and by the time they hung up, Abby seemed to have forgotten about the contaminated-food theory.

Susannah hadn't. It was still there, lurking in her brain, a tiny thought dressed in a dark cape and hat, intent on spoiling her day.

Take your own advice, she ordered. Forget it. We've been hosting this Memorial Day bash for twelve years, and not once in all that time has anyone fallen ill from the food. Old Mrs. Bannister did faint one year, but that was because she was wearing a long-sleeved jacket on a day when the temperature was over ninety, and Sam fell out of a tree when he was watching the fire-works, but that was his own fault.

There had never, *ever* been anything wrong with the food.

And there won't be today, Susannah thought emphatically, moving to one of two walk-in closets to grab something to wear to Emsee. Unless her mother really needed her this morning, she *was* going to volunteer for a few hours. If it was really quiet and she wasn't needed, she could check on Toni, and see if Jeremy was still glued to a chair in the ICU waiting room.

Before she went downstairs, she called Will. He was, he said, feeling "terrific," and planned to arrive at Linden Hall around two.

Susannah was smiling when she hung up.

Although her mother expressed reservations about her daughter leaving on such a hectic morning, she didn't insist that Susannah stay home.

Toni was no better, no worse than she had been the night before. Her blood tests had shown nothing enlightening, but she was "stable." Jeremy hadn't left the hospital at all, but the night nurse had talked him into sacking out on the leather couch in the waiting room, and he had slept a little. Disheveled and bleary-eyed when Susannah woke him, he looked exhausted.

When Susannah told him that Callie had called and said she wasn't feeling well, Jeremy looked stricken. "Oh, god," he cried, "she was at my party, too!"

"Jeremy, it's got nothing to do with that." Susannah sat down beside him. "Will wasn't at your party, and neither was Julie Whittier. It's something else." While she meant what she was saying, it occurred to her then that she wasn't necessarily being accurate. If the food that Will had eaten was part of a large shipment, as she'd theorized to Abby, *some* of that same shipment might well have ended up at Jeremy's house.

But then, why hadn't *all* of the guests fallen ill like Toni and Callie?

Tired of theorizing, Susannah pushed the matter out of her mind and set about trying to convince Jeremy to come to the picnic. "You can't do anymore for Toni here. She's resting comfortably. Why not come, have a good time, and then you can come back here later? They might know something more about her condition by then. Come on, Jeremy, you can't stay here all day."

When he had finally agreed to meet her out front at the end of her shift, Susannah went downstairs to the E.R.

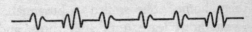

"**N**o word on the Duval boy, or on the Whittier girl's cause of death." Astrid handed Susannah a clipboard with admissions forms attached. "In the Duval case, Dr. Maclaine still thinks it was poison, but the blood tests haven't told us anything definitive. The boy is still in ICU."

"Have you had any more cases of . . . summer complaint?" Susannah was thinking of Callie. "Callie Matthews didn't come in, did she?"

Astrid's mouth turned downward. "Bite your tongue! It's a gorgeous day. Why ruin it with a visit from Miss Matthews? And no, we haven't had any more stomach cases, except for an emergency appendectomy, came in around seven-twenty, and it really *was* the appendix. Sent him upstairs to surgery. But that's it, so far."

That was good news. No more new cases. And maybe Callie had recovered. Either that or she'd medicated herself, with heaven only knew what.

"According to the log," Astrid continued, "it stayed fairly quiet in here last night after you left. Two car wrecks, no deaths, and three cardiacs, all surviving over at Cardiopulmonary. Not bad, I'd say. The two migraines we had here yesterday came back, though. Stomach problems. But," she added hastily, "that's common, because of all the medication they take. We treated them and sent them home." She smiled at Susannah. "I heard you didn't leave until after three, and I came on at seven. That doesn't leave a lot of time for mayhem. Girl, you must be wiped."

"Not really. You're coming up to the picnic after work, right?"

"I wouldn't miss it." The smile widened into a grin identical to Kate's. "I'll bet things are hopping up there on the hill, am I right?"

"You're right. It looks great. I wish Kate were coming for the picnic. She's not planning to show up until late, for the fireworks, and she didn't even sound too sure about that."

"Maybe she'll change her mind. Now, how about trotting out to the waiting room and bringing me that foolish young boy who had a run-in with a firecracker. You can't miss him. He's the one with a blood-stained T-shirt wrapped around his left thumb and forefinger. They're still attached to his hand, because he got lucky, but he needs stitches. Maclaine will do it. She's filling in for Mulgrew today. Suture Room B."

Susannah didn't talk to the doctor while the

stitching took place, but when the patient, after a brief lecture from the physician, had gone, she asked if there had been any news on the Duval boy.

The pediatrician's face darkened. "Nothing yet. What worries me," she added as she pushed away from the table, "is if those lab people know what they're looking for. Some poisons don't show up unless you're actually hunting for them."

"What kind of poison do you think they should be looking for?"

"I'm not sure."

Yeah, she is, Susannah thought emphatically. She's just not ready to say.

Just then, Astrid's voice called out, "Train–car collision on railroad tracks! Six victims, two iffy. All personnel to emergency entrance, stat!"

Susannah and the doctor ran from the room. There was no more talk of poison.

The next hour strained the emergency center to its limits. The injuries from the terrible crash were all serious. Two were life-threatening. Not only did those two patients have severe head injuries, there were broken bones and, in one case, an open chest wound as well. Susannah always wondered, in such multi-injury cases, how the doctors decided which area to treat first.

Gurneys and orderlies, doctors and nurses and

nurse's aides, raced from room to room. One patient stopped breathing on the table. Susannah and an orderly raced to that room with the crash cart. Both stood clear as the paddles applied electrical stimulation to the endangered heart. Sometimes it worked, sometimes it didn't. This time, it did.

But there were still open fractures to be closed and set, lacerations to be stitched shut, IV's to set up, blood pressure to be monitored. The head injury cases required immediate CAT scans. Susannah helped escort the gurneys upstairs in the elevator for those special X rays, and carted other, less seriously injured patients to X ray for more ordinary films.

Every patient was still breathing as they were taken from Emergency.

"Well, we didn't lose any," Astrid said as the last patient was wheeled away to a room upstairs, "but I'd like to get my hands on the idiot who drove that car into a freight train! He hadn't been drinking, either. None of them had. He was just plain stupid. I'd bet this month's salary they were racing that train."

"Their idea of holiday entertainment." Dr. Izbecki looked exhausted, his face lined and drawn. "I can't believe they all made it. Eight people in a car that hit a freight train going seventy miles an hour, and they all survive. That knocks me out."

"They haven't all survived *yet*," Astrid pointed out. "The next twenty-four hours will tell the story. I wouldn't take any bets on that head-and-chest injury making it. His mother nearly fainted when she saw him. I thought we were going to lose *her*."

Although the E.R. fell quiet for a while, and Susannah looked around for Dr. Maclaine, hoping to continue their earlier conversation, she saw no sign of the pediatrician.

She told herself that no one knew for certain that *any* poison was actually in the boy's system. She told herself that even if it were, it could have been ingested accidentally. It was spring. There were lawn-care company vans driving all over the city, these days, spraying gardens and lawns. And then she reminded herself sternly that Dr. Maclaine's theory about poison was just that, a theory. Without tests to back up her theory, she couldn't possibly be positive.

So why even think about it? It was pointless, a waste of energy. Might as well wait and find out the truth, whatever it was, when everyone else did.

That decision should have granted Susannah some peace of mind. But it didn't.

When she left at one-thirty, Jeremy was waiting for her, as promised. He wasn't in a very good mood.

"Toni's not any better," he said heavily. "Why can't they do something to help her?"

"Because they're not sure what's wrong with her."

"They're *supposed* to know!"

"They're doctors, Jeremy, not psychics. But they'll figure it out. Soon. And they'll fix it."

Susannah hoped she was right.

Susannah and her mother had their annual argument about proper attire for the picnic. Susannah voted for shorts and a tank top, while her mother pushed the royal-blue sundress she had brought home from Madoline's, a chic boutique in town, earlier in the week. "It's the same color as your eyes. That's why I bought it. You'll look adorable."

"Babies are adorable, Mother. I'm not a baby. I don't want to look adorable. I want to be cool and comfortable."

They finally compromised. Susannah would wear shorts during the day, changing into the sundress for the evening festivities. She decided she liked the idea of Will seeing her in that dress. It really was gorgeous. She would have to be absolutely sure she removed Madoline's elegant little pink price tag. If Will ever saw the number of zeroes in the dollar amount, they'd need a crash cart to resuscitate him.

When she went outside, she found her mother calm, Tish nervously racing from table to table checking last-minute details, and her father complaining that one of the six waiters he'd hired to circulate through the crowd with trays of drinks, hadn't arrived yet. If they saw him, the three women were told, they were to send him to the picnic site immediately. "It's always something," Samuel Grant murmured absentmindedly as he left to check the fireworks setup one last time. "Is it so much to ask that employees show up when they say they will?"

Susannah and her mother exchanged an amused glance. "He gets like this every year," Caroline Grant said. "I keep telling him, it's just a picnic, but you know your father. If things are to be done properly, he has to see to them himself."

That makes two of you, Susannah thought, but she thought it with affection.

People began arriving shortly before two o'clock. Linden Hill was quickly lined on both sides with cars, trucks, and vans. Abby and Sid arrived in one of the specially equipped Rehab vans that Sid had recently begun driving on outings from his hospital room. Susannah, waiting on the front terrace for Will, helped Abby unload the wheelchair.

"Sid, you have *got* to be in the tug-of-war," Susannah commented as he settled into the chair. "All those workouts you hate so much at Rehab have really done the trick. With those arms and shoulders, your team would destroy the other guys."

Sid's handsome, olive skin flushed with pleasure, but he shook his head. "No way. These wheels might run over someone and pulverize them. But I could deal with tossing a few horseshoes. Abby said you have a pit." He grinned at Abby, looking cool and pretty in a pink romper. "She also said she's lousy at horseshoes, so I plan to pulverize *her*. A few perfectly aimed tosses, and she'll go down in defeat."

"Coming, Susannah?" Abby called as she began steering the chair up the side walkway toward the rear of the house.

"Nope. Waiting for Will. Have fun!"

She had just about decided he wasn't going to show when his truck came around the last curve at the top of the hill. She ran down the steps to direct him to the only parking place left in the circular driveway. If it occurred to him that his weather-beaten red truck stuck out in the midst of all those Cadillacs and Jaguars and Mercedes, he didn't comment on it.

He looked great, in khaki shorts and a white knit short-sleeved shirt that showed off his build. He also looked perfectly healthy, which was a relief to Susannah.

"Feeling okay?" she asked as he jumped from the truck.

"Never better." He draped an arm around

her shoulders as they walked toward the house.

Her parents had met Will twice before. But both those encounters had been during emergency situations, and she was fairly sure they hadn't been paying much attention. This would be the first time they'd met in a strictly social setting. Still, all of her life her parents had refused to allow even the slightest hint of racism in any conversation, joke, or statement. She wasn't worried. Not *really* worried.

They followed the wide stone pathway around the house to the picnic site. The hilltop was alive with activity. The crystal-clear waters of the pool rang with the shouts of swimmers and divers. To their right, a steady *thwack-thwack* of tennis balls sounded from the courts. Men were still working on the fireworks display at the far end of the hill, while opposite them, a group of guests, including Abby and Sid, tossed horseshoes. In the flower-bedecked gazebo, she caught glimpses of people dancing to the upbeat music that provided a background to the laughter and conversation.

When Will spotted Damon, wearing a white jacket and holding high a round white tray, weaving his way among the guests, he surprised Susannah by saying in disgust, "Oh, man! I can't believe he actually *did* it! I thought I'd talked him out of it."

Puzzled, Susannah followed his eyes and saw

Damon. "You tried to talk him out of working here today? Why would you do that? Kate said he needed the extra money."

Will's mouth twisted. "Seein' him in that white coat, taking orders from people who make more money in a year than my old man made in his whole life, makes me want to puke."

Irritation, mixed with hurt, rose in Susannah. "He's *not* taking orders. He carries the trays around with drinks or canapes on them, and people take what they want. And besides, everyone here isn't rich. Lots of people here are clerks and secretaries and lab technicians, teachers at Grant U . . . this isn't one of my parents' private dinner parties, Will."

He'd been gazing out across the picnic scene. Now he turned quickly, his expression repentant. "I'm a jerk. Hey, I'm sorry. Look, this is a good thing your parents do every year. Everyone says so. I just . . . I hate to see Damon playing waiter, that's all. But," he shrugged, "if he's cool about it, I guess I am, too." He reached out a hand to lift her chin and force her eyes to meet his. "You mad?"

"Um . . . I don't know. Maybe. Depends."

Will looked wary. "On what?"

"On whether or not you're going to dance with me in the gazebo before it gets too crowded."

"Can do. Lead the way."

They were halfway down the wide, stone steps when a man in a black jacket approached them. Susannah recognized him as the headwaiter, the man in charge of the six waitpersons. He looked annoyed. Her heartbeat skidded to a halt. Will . . . the tardy waiter. . . . No, no, the man wasn't going to . . .

But he did. "About time!" The man was looking directly at Will and extended a white, long-sleeved jacket identical to the one Damon was wearing. "You were supposed to be here at one-thirty. I do not appreciate tardiness, nor does Mr. Grant." Thrusting the jacket into Will's hands, he turned to point to Tish, standing in a group of guests near the gazebo. "Go to that woman over there. She'll give you instructions."

Susannah was horrified. This man thought Will was one of the *waiters*!

Will's face was thunderous.

"You're making a terrible mistake," she said hastily, knowing her face was deepening in color. "I'm Susannah Grant and this," trying to take Will's hand and failing because he pulled away from her, "is a guest. *My* guest. You owe him an apology."

The man gasped, and paled. "Oh, oh, Miss Grant, I am *so* sorry. But," he turned to point again, this time to Damon, "that young man over there said the other waiter was a friend of his, so I naturally assumed . . ."

"You naturally assumed it was me," Will said smoothly. He held up the white jacket, as if he were checking it for size. "Whadya think, Susannah? I might look pretty hot in this, know what I mean?"

"No," Susannah said, conscious of his anger. "You wouldn't look good in it at all, Will. Give it back to the man. Will," she said quietly, "please don't do this. This man has apologized."

"To *you*," Will said darkly. "He has apologized to you. Not to me."

Picking up on the cue, the headwaiter said, "I am truly sorry, sir. Please, you have my deepest regrets."

Will turned to look at Susannah. Before she could stop him, he loped on down the steps and made his way through the crowd, his back and broad shoulders very straight.

chapter
19

—⩗⩗⩗⩗⩗⩗⩗⩗—

Tired of horseshoes, Abby and Sid came looking for Susannah. They found her on her way to watch the tug-of-war. The first thing Abby asked her was, "Where's Will?"

Susannah explained as they moved into the center of the lawn where two teams of ten people each had gathered.

Abby and Sid shared Susannah's horror over the mistake the headwaiter had made. "God, Will must feel terrible! You should go find him."

Susannah knew Abby was right. She had to find him, tell him how sorry she was, make him give in.

"Okay, I'll . . . "

Suddenly, Abby's mouth dropped open as she caught sight of something behind Susannah, and shock appeared in her eyes. "Oh, my god, what is *wrong* with Callie? Susannah, *look* at her! There, by the cabana."

Grateful to be off the subject of Will, Susannah said as she turned around to look, "She's sick, remember? I told you she called me this morning. Wanted me to play pharmacist."

"You said she was sick. You didn't say she looked like a zombie. What's wrong with her?"

Susannah frowned as a flush of guilt washed over her. Was Callie really seriously ill? "Maybe I should have done more than I did," she said slowly, watching as Callie, looking dazed, moved along the picnic site, one hand on her stomach, the other grasping one object after another for support. Susannah continued to watch as the searching hand traveled from a tree trunk to a table to a chair to a tall, potted plant beside the cabana, then to the doorknob of the poolhouse. Callie staggered when the door opened, and then disappeared inside. "I should have called one of her parents, told them she was sick. But I didn't have a clue that she was in such a bad way." She turned back to Abby. "We should do something."

Abby nodded. "Right. But what?"

"Well, for one thing, we can keep her out of the pool. If she went into the cabana to change into her bathing suit, she must be planning on diving in. The shape she's in, she's sure to drown. Look, could you do me a favor, you guys? I need to find Will, straighten things out with him. I have to. Could you guys go find Callie and keep her out of that pool? If Will's speaking to me, I'll bring him over. If he won't come, I'll grab a doctor."

Abby nodded. "Gotcha! But hurry, okay? If she gets away from me and I have to dive in after her, I'll give new meaning to the phrase, 'bad hair day.'"

Susannah ran to get help.

chapter
20

Inside the cabana, Abby argued, "Callie, swimming would be just about the dumbest thing you could do right now. Are you nuts? I know you're a terrific swimmer, but even a fish can die in the water if it's too sick to swim."

They were alone. Sid had agreed to wait outside in his wheelchair, partly because Callie was in the women's side of the large poolhouse, and partly because he really didn't care if Callie Matthews drowned. He might not be a rocket scientist, but he'd figured out a long time ago that Callie thought Abby was weird for being with him. Callie understood *nothing*. Let her drown.

Abby wasn't getting anywhere, until she got unexpected help from Callie herself, who was simply incapable of removing her clothes to change into her bathing suit.

With great effort, she lifted her head. Eyes full of desperation and confusion fixed on Abby's face. "Help me," she whispered, "help me, Abby!"

Abby had hardened her heart to Callie long ago. One thing she couldn't tolerate was meanness of spirit, and Callie had that in spades. While Abby and her entire family were grateful that Callie had saved Carmel and Geneva from raging flood waters, that gratitude had quickly worn thin when Callie went right back to her old, evil ways.

But this pale, pathetic creature weaving unsteadily in front of her now seemed perfectly harmless, and seriously in need of help. And Susannah hadn't returned yet, with or without Will. "Sit down," Abby commanded, and led Callie to a padded bench. "I'm getting a doctor. I'll be right back. Don't move, you hear me?"

Hands pressing against her stomach, Callie nodded.

"Don't let her out of there," Abby warned Sid as she left the cabana in search of help.

"Oh, no problem," Sid said with just a hint of irritation. Callie was spoiling his good time. "If she splits, I'll just jump right out of this chair and race after her. Might even tackle her if I have to."

"Very funny, Costello. Just keep her here, okay? Maybe I should look for Callie's dad. He must be around somewhere. But first, I need to dig up a doctor."

Sid laughed. "Now *there's* a challenge. Half the

staff of Emsee must be here. If you yell for a doctor, you'll be stampeded."

Patsy Keene, standing nearby in a group that included Bobs Swickert, Connie Brewer, and Greta Schwinn, overheard Abby. "Callie's dad isn't here," she called out. "He was, a little while ago. But then he got a phone call. Something about a crisis situation at Med Center."

"I'll bet it's about that Whittier girl," Greta Schwinn, in a lemon-yellow linen sheath, said. "Her parents are *not* happy. And it's not just losing their daughter that's rattled them. They don't like the way the postmortem is being handled, either. Probably threatening to sue Emsee. Caleb wouldn't like that, not at all."

Abby would have liked to join in the conversation. She was interested in anything that was going on at Med Center. But Callie needed help, and she needed it now.

Helene Maclaine was the first doctor Abby encountered. Looking very attractive in a white pantsuit, she was sitting poolside, drink in hand, talking animatedly to Astrid, who had just arrived. Abby was happy to see Kate, in shorts and a tank top, her hair cornrowed, standing just behind her mother.

"Susannah said you weren't coming," Abby said as she joined them. "I'm glad you changed your mind." Remembering why she was there, she turned quickly and explained the situation to Dr. Maclaine. "Can you take a look at Callie? She's really a mess."

Astrid and Kate came with them to the pool-house. On the way there, Abby couldn't stop herself from saying, "I know everyone says that Julie Whittier died of complications from surgery, but if you ask me, Callie's symptoms are the same as Julie's. I helped Susannah transport Julie into one of the cubicles, and I remember she looked exactly the way Callie looks now. I think there's something contagious going around."

Dr. Maclaine gave her a long, penetrating look. "Don't repeat that," she said in a level voice. "The hospital's in enough trouble right now, with all the questions about Whittier. There is *no* evidence that we're dealing with a contagion. None."

"Then what *is* it?" Abby asked, her voice rising.

"That's for the hospital to discover."

When they reached the cabana, Sid was gone. And so was Callie.

"Talk to me," Susannah told Will in a voice that left little room for argument. She had finally found him sitting near the cliff overlooking Med Center. He was staring angrily down upon the valley. Settling beside him, she repeated, "I'm

sorry, Will. I'm sorry it happened. But the guy is an idiot, that's all."

"Things like this happen too often," Will said.

"Look, Will, Callie is sick. Really sick. She might need to go to Emsee. You're a paramedic. Will you please come check her out? I think she's got what you had yesterday. If you think she needs to go to the E.R., we'll take her, okay? And while she's being examined, we can talk," Susannah said.

He looked at her then. "Callie? She was fine last night, at Jeremy's party."

"Well, she isn't now. She looks like death. Abby went looking for a doctor, and I want to get back there and see what's happening. They're at the poolhouse. Are you coming?"

She saw his hesitation, knew what he was thinking. He didn't like Callie, and there were plenty of other people at the picnic qualified to help a sick girl. And he was probably also thinking, why should he help *anyone*?

Susannah wasn't willing to give up yet. "Please, Will? Callie will let you check her out before she'll let a doctor near her. She knows they'll tell her father she's sick."

He jumped up then, began striding away, without asking her to come with him.

Susannah caught up quickly, hurrying along beside him.

"She's gone," Abby said when they arrived. Sid

159

was there, in his wheelchair, and Helene Maclaine, looking exasperated. And Kate.

Susannah was glad to see Kate. But at the moment, Callie was on her mind. "Gone?" Susannah echoed. "Gone where?"

"It's my fault," Sid said with only a minimal amount of contrition. "Abby asked me to keep her here. Then Jeremy showed up, crying on my shoulder about that girl from the party last night. Toni Barnes? I guess I wasn't watching the door, and Callie sneaked by me. I looked for her, but she's disappeared. Sorry."

Susannah glanced around. The picnic was in full swing now, the hilltop swarming with people intent on having a good time. She saw many red outfits . . . shorts, skirts, pantsuits, and sundresses, but none of them was being worn by Callie Matthews. "Oh, god," she murmured. "The pool!" She was breaking into a run even before she finished the thought.

She was halfway there, the rest of the group a few feet behind her, when she spotted Callie's red outfit. Callie wasn't in the pool, floating facedown as she'd dreaded. She wasn't in the pool at all. Callie hadn't gone swimming. She had, instead, joined the tug-of-war.

There were two teams. Callie was the second person on one team of ten people.

"Can you believe this?" Susannah cried, stopping short. "When I left her, she was reeling.

Now look at her!" Then she realized exactly *why* Callie had opted for the tug-of-war instead of the pool. The person directly in front of her was Sam. He was tugging with all of his considerable might, his handsome face strained with the exertion. And Lily Dolan was nowhere in sight.

Callie had seen an opportunity, and seized it.

Susannah and the others watched in silence for several moments.

"How sick can she be?" Dr. Maclaine asked, her eyes on Callie. Of Abby, she asked, "Could you have been mistaken? Maybe she was faking. Callie Matthews, right? I've heard stories about her. An attention-getter. Maybe she was just yanking your chain."

"No," Susannah said quickly. "I saw her, too. She is really sick."

"She is," Dr. Maclaine said, "upright and breathing at this particular moment. I repeat, how sick can she be?" Replacing her sunglasses, she added, "Feel free to fetch me if you have a *genuine* emergency." She patted the black beeper clinging to her leather belt like a baby possum. "Unless I get a call about the Duval boy, I intend to enjoy the festivities. I'll see all of you later. Have fun!"

She had taken no more than two steps when Callie suddenly let go of the rope. Both hands flew to her stomach. Susannah could see her face twisting and knew what was coming. Sam, not realizing what had happened, was caught off-guard when the rope went slack behind him. He lost his balance and his grip.

Callie's knees folded like paper. She was on the way down when the opposing team felt or saw a weakening in the pull on the rope, and moved in for the kill. They didn't see what was happening to Callie. All they knew was, this was their chance. They took it. Putting all of their strength behind the pull, they yanked, hard.

Callie was lying on the ground on her back, her hands on her stomach, when the other eight members of her team were propelled rapidly forward by the sudden, powerful yank on the rope.

Susannah, seeing what was about to happen, screamed a warning. But no one heard her over all of the shouting and taunting.

If Sam hadn't turned his head, seen Callie lying on the ground, and thrown up his hands as a warning, Callie would have been trampled to death.

As it was, a sudden stop when eight people were being dragged rapidly forward at the same time, would have been impossible. In the effort to avoid the fallen girl, people tumbled over one another like bowling pins. Susannah saw the tip of a sneaker strike Callie in the back of the skull, saw a bended knee land on her shoulder, felt the blow when another foot slammed into her upper right arm. With each blow, her body jerked. Susannah was reminded of unconscious patients being revived by the crash-cart paddles.

Spectators who had gathered to watch the tug-of-war made sounds . . . gasps of horror, cries of alarm, calls for help, but it all mixed in with the noise of other groups completely unaware of what was taking place.

Dr. Maclaine was already running to the jumbled spill of people.

Susannah, Will, and Abby were right behind her, and Sid was wheeling his chair as fast as their feet were flying.

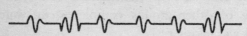

It amazed Susannah that the only serious injury as a result of the melee was Callie's. Dr. Maclaine determined very quickly that Callie had probably suffered a concussion when the foot struck her skull. She was unconscious, her eyes closed, her body limp.

Susannah, watching with Abby, Sid, and Kate, wondered if that really was from the blow, or if Callie had lost consciousness from her illness before the foot ever struck her.

At the first sign of disaster, Caroline Grant, cellular telephone in hand, had called for an ambulance. While they waited for its arrival, Dr. Maclaine and two other physicians, both in casual wear and carrying the black bags that were always with them, checked the other team members. Some of the victims were still sprawled on the lawn.

"They don't know what hit them," Will commented.

"Chaos is what hit them," Kate said. "What

happened, anyway? I see Callie over there. That mess is *her* doing? Figures."

Susannah explained. A crowd was gathering, so she kept her voice low. If she said too much in public about Callie's sudden sickness being similar to Julie's, people might panic. They'd remember last summer's virus and worry that it was happening all over again. Hadn't she wondered the same thing herself?

"Callie's sick?" Damon asked as he approached. "All of that meanness she carries around inside her must have finally poisoned her."

Funny you should mention poison, Abby thought, thinking of Bradley Duval.

"You still haven't told me why Callie collapsed," Kate said.

Abby spoke up before Susannah had a chance to answer. "She wasn't feeling so great, but she did the tug-of-war anyway. I guess the heat got to her. Then someone accidentally kicked her."

Kate's answering look was skeptical. "I know all that. Susannah already explained. I meant, if what Callie has isn't serious, why did she collapse in the first place?"

A couple standing slightly behind Abby was listening carefully. They've seen us volunteering at Med Center, she realized, and they're thinking we must know something they don't.

They're hoping to hear what that something is.

The scream of an arriving ambulance saved Abby from answering Kate's question.

Dr. Maclaine rode along with Callie in the ambulance. Susannah offered to go, too, but was waved away. "Don't be silly. Stay and enjoy your picnic. Her father's at the hospital, and I'll notify him by radio that she's on her way. He'll be with her. Really, Susannah, go on now, have fun."

Susannah tried. When the ambulance had departed, the picnic quickly got back into full swing. Callie Matthews didn't have enough fans to cast a pall over the festivities, and anyone who might have been concerned about her knew that she was in good hands. The band began playing again. The sound of clanging metal rang out from the horseshoe pit, and the team that had won the tug-of-war tossed the losers into the pool.

After only a few minutes, there was no sign that anything had gone wrong at Caroline and Samuel Grant's annual Memorial Day bash.

After his dunking, Sam went inside to don dry clothing. Then he and Lily headed for the tennis courts. Damon took a ten-minute break from his duties as waiter to sit at one of the tables with Kate. Jeremy went into the house to call Med Center and inquire about Toni, and Susannah, after seeing the ambulance off, changed into the cobalt blue dress. She returned to the picnic site wishing the day was at an end and everyone had gone home. It was only five-thirty. Hours to go still before she could curl up on the windowseat in her room and try to figure out how things had turned so sour.

She met Tish on her way out of the house. Her arms were filled with cardboard boxes.

"You're not going home already, are you?" Susannah asked, taking the top box.

"Nope. Just bringing these boxes inside."

Susannah took one of the boxes and held the door open for Tish. "Are you having fun?" Susannah asked. They plopped the boxes down on the kitchen counter.

"Sure!" It sounded forced. "Why not? Good food, good weather, good people. What happened to that friend of yours? Someone said she got kicked in the head? How did that happen?"

Susannah told the story again.

"Gruesome! But you said she was sick? Shouldn't have been partying if she was sick. I hope it wasn't anything catching." Tish withdrew a clean glass from the kitchen cupboard and filled it with water and ice from the refrigerator door. "Man, I'm wiped out!" she said when she had sipped thirstily. "But, except for that disaster with your friend, this party has been the best so far. A couple more like this and I can quit that stupid job at the lab."

"And get married and have kids," Susannah

said without thinking, but to her surprise, Tish only smiled. "Yep. Kids and marriage. Next on the agenda. C'mon, let's get back out there before all the food's gone."

Susannah followed her out, so when they were standing on the rear veranda, she was close enough to hear Tish gasp and whisper, "Oh, no! I thought he was out of town."

When Susannah followed Tish's dismayed stare, she saw Dr. Barlow standing at the side of the house, surveying the picnic scene. And he wasn't alone.

"Oh, of *course* he had to bring someone with him!" Tish said bitterly. "Twist the knife a little, why don't you, Tom?"

The woman with him was a petite blond who, to Susannah's eyes, strongly resembled Nurse Patsy Keene. But this woman was dressed smartly in a white linen suit, with red heels and clutch bag, and her hair was styled in a sophisticated upsweep. Patsy was cute, but when she wasn't on duty at Grant Memorial, she ran around town in jeans and T-shirts, denim jackets and sneakers.

"Patsy Keene with a makeover," Tish grumbled at Susannah's side, as if she'd been reading her thoughts. "Patsy must be fuming. It's almost as if Tom brought that woman here to say, See, Patsy, you could look like this if you wanted, and then maybe I wouldn't have dumped you. Except, of course, he would have. He'll dump this one, too, sooner or later."

Susannah's eyes moved into the crowd until she found the trio of nurses. Patsy, Bobs, and Greta, were all staring at the veranda as Susannah had expected. Their expressions varied. Patsy's was blatantly angry. Greta's eyes looked hurt and confused. It was clear that neither had expected Dr. Barlow to show up, and certainly not with a strange woman. Only Bobs appeared calm, but Susannah knew Bobs wasn't easily upset, and when she was, she didn't show it. She kept her emotions to herself.

And here came Jeremy, moving through the crowd to approach the parent he hadn't expected to see. He should look happy, Susannah thought, still watching from the side of the house. His father had come, after all. But happy was not how Jeremy looked. The fierce scowl on his face told Susannah that he would have preferred his father not show up at all.

As Jeremy sullenly greeted his father and guest, Tish turned away and said with false cheerfulness, "Did you know I grew most of these flowers myself, Susannah? The hydrangeas, anyway," pointing to a massive display of pink and blue blossoms in baskets on each side of the wide, stone steps. "Saves me a fortune in florist's fees. I don't have to use a florist at all except for huge parties like your parents'. And gardening is such great therapy." Her tone changed again. "For those who *need* it!"

"Tish . . ."

"Well, back to work! Have fun, Susie-Q. See ya later." When she reached the bottom of the steps, Tish deliberately turned sharply left to avoid confronting Dr. Barlow, then walked across the thick grass to the gazebo.

Annoyed at this new glitch in her plans for a fun day, Susannah sent a sharp glance in Dr. Barlow's direction. He wasn't looking at her. He was watching Tish.

Yes, she *does* look gorgeous today, Susannah messaged him mentally, so what are you doing with someone else?

When she didn't see Will anywhere, Susannah went to borrow her mother's cell phone to call the hospital. But when she inquired about Callie's condition, she was told only, "Unless you're a relative, we can't give out that information. You probably should call her family instead."

I'll go to Med Center after the fireworks, Susannah decided after she'd hung up. I have to know how Callie is, and what's wrong with her.

She was about to turn around when warm, strong hands covered her eyes. "Don't guess who this is," Will's deep voice said from behind her. " 'Cause if you guess right, you might decide to slam an elbow into my ribs. I'll say I'm sorry just this one time. Just once. If you decide you're cool with that, turn around. If you don't turn around in the next sixty seconds, I'm out of here, and that's okay, too."

As if she needed sixty seconds.

chapter
22

The fireworks display, everyone said, was the best ever. Abby and Sid had taken seats on the white wicker swing on the veranda, while Susannah and Will sat on the steps, their hands clasped together. Sam and Lily were right behind them, in wicker chairs. Kate and Damon had chosen to stay in the pool, and watched from there as the dark sky above Linden Hall blazed gold and silver, red and orange, blue and green.

A thoroughly disgruntled Jeremy had left earlier. His mumbled excuse to Susannah was that he had a headache. But she suspected he wanted to get as far away from his father and the white-suited blond woman as possible.

Although it was late when the last trace of fiery glow fizzled and died, Susannah announced as the guests began to leave that she was off to Med Center to see how Callie was. "Anyone want to come?"

Will had already planned to take a run over to the complex and see how busy it was. If it was really hectic, he planned to volunteer on a few ambulance runs, giving the on-duty paramedics the chance for a quick cup of coffee. Lily and Sam weren't interested in anything but each other, and Kate's answer was to give Susannah a cynical look, as if to say, Why would I care how Callie is?

"I guess it's just you and me," Susannah said, turning to Will.

He grinned. "You don't hear me complaining, do you?"

Tish and her staff had just begun the clean-up when Susannah's Benz and Will's truck pulled away from Linden Hall.

Except for the headwaiter's mistake, the tug-of-war incident, and Dr. Barlow's sudden appearance, the picnic had been fun, Susannah decided as she steered the car around Linden Hill's snake-like curves.

No one at the picnic had seemed to think anything of Susannah and Will openly holding hands, dancing in the gazebo, sitting close together during the fireworks display. There had been a few curious looks, she'd seen those. They hadn't bothered her. And her parents, always a class act, had introduced Will to a great many of their friends.

Maybe Will would relax a little now. They'd made it through an entire day in public together without the sky falling or the earth opening up and swallowing them.

Now if only Callie was okay. Pain in the neck or not, Susannah didn't like the idea of anyone at their picnic ending up in the hospital, and she knew her parents were concerned, too. And *they* hadn't seen the state Julie Whittier was in when she came into the E.R. If they had, and realized how similar Callie's condition was, they'd be freaking now.

When she pulled into Med Center's driveway, it hit her again how much she loved the place. Arriving here always made her feel like she was coming home. The picnic had been fun, but she'd missed her usual Sunday-afternoon stint in the E.R. She had finals all this week, and would have very little time for volunteer work.

But then she had the whole summer ahead of her. She could work every day if she felt like it. Her parents would have a fit, telling her to go out and "play," like her twin, while she was still young. But they wouldn't order her to quit her volunteer work. They knew better.

Greta Schwinn was the night head nurse in the E.R. Because Susannah had noticed the crowded waiting room as she entered the building, she wasn't surprised when Nurse Schwinn, who had just come on duty, greeted her with, "I have never been so glad to see anyone in my life! I didn't know you were coming. Thank you, thank you, thank you!" She shoved a clipboard at Susannah. "Good thing tomorrow's a holiday.

No school, right? Because I have to warn you, I may need you here all night. But you can sleep tomorrow, okay?"

Susannah had planned to spend most of the day cramming for finals. But she could sleep all morning and study when she got up.

"Patsy and Bobs are here, too," Greta went on hurriedly, "but it's been a madhouse. I just came on, and couldn't believe what they've been going through over here. All kinds of river accidents . . ." Her expression sobered. "Two drownings. Izbecki tried everything, but it was too late. An eight-year-old boy and his ten-year-old sister. Their mother was so hysterical, she had to be admitted. She's upstairs, under heavy sedation. And so far, there have been at least a dozen accidents with firecrackers. Two kids had to be transported to the Burn Unit. One's going to be scarred for sure, and the other one might lose the hearing in his left ear." Her lips tightened in disapproval. "He was only five. Someone *gave* him those firecrackers, someone old enough to know better. People never learn."

"Where do you want me?" Although Susannah hadn't been sure she would be needed, she had brought her pink smock. She slipped it on over her clothes and snatched a pen from the holder on the admissions desk. "In the waiting room, taking info?"

"Yep. Patsy's in the suture room and Bobs just

took another gastro case upstairs. Same symptoms as Callie Matthews. Not as bad, though. Fifteen-year-old. Mother said he'd been having headaches lately." The nurse glanced down at the notes on her desk. "Family doctor thought it might be meningitis, but the stomach thing doesn't fit. Lobell's taking a look at him."

"Have you heard how Callie is?"

"Nope. Haven't had time to ask. It can wait, can't it?" Lifting her head and inclining it toward the waiting room, Greta Schwinn added, "I really need you out there. The minute there's a lull, you can call upstairs and see how your friend is."

Susannah didn't take the time to correct the nurse and point out that she wasn't sure she would call Callie a *friend.* She wasn't sure what she *would* call her. I guess, Susannah thought as she hurried to the waiting room, I just think of Callie as someone I know and usually wish I didn't. But I still don't want her to end up like Julie Whittier.

But it was a long time before she was free to call upstairs and inquire about Callie's condition.

There were two more near-drownings, an older couple who had decided to take a midnight canoe ride. Because neither one had negotiated a canoe in over thirty years, they weren't in the river's swift current ten minutes before their boat overturned. They were swept downriver in water

176

that was still chilly from the winter. Too cold to swim, they would have drowned quickly if a group of eight young people celebrating on the riverbank hadn't seen them speeding by, arms flailing, crying out for help. Three had jumped in to help, while others in the group alerted authorities.

The man, who had a heart condition, had been transferred to Cardiopulmonary following his emergency treatment. The woman had emerged the luckier of the two, in good enough condition to accompany his gurney as it was wheeled through the glass-enclosed passageways leading from Grant Memorial to other buildings in the complex.

Susannah had just begun volunteering the preceding July Fourth, and had seen firecracker injuries during that holiday weekend almost a year ago. But none had been as serious as the four teenagers who were brought in around two o'clock. They'd been drunk, and fooling around with lit firecrackers. The firecrackers had gone off in the kids' faces.

Their screams were horrible, and Susannah, called in from the waiting room to help, was thoroughly sickened by the damage. They might as well have thrust their heads into an open flame.

Every available doctor was called to the E.R.

Patsy, Bobs, and Greta saw to comforting the patients while their burns were examined. Susannah ran to gather extra bottles of saline solution, and gauze pads. As she ran, she prayed the four would be sedated quickly and heavily. It was the only thing that would stop their screaming.

When the medication was given and took effect, a grateful silence fell over the first floor of Grant Memorial. Susannah could almost hear the sighs of relief. There had to be people in the waiting room whose relatively minor aches and pains suddenly didn't seem quite so bad, after hearing what they'd heard and seeing what they must have seen when the gurneys raced by them.

When the last of the four had been moved to the Burn Hospital, there was a brief lull in activity. Susannah took advantage of it to move to the admissions desk to call upstairs and ask about Callie.

"Not here," she was told. "Upstairs, ICU. I wouldn't call up there, though. They've got their hands full. Wait till morning, that's the best idea."

Callie had been taken to ICU? That meant she was worse. A lot worse. Like Julie Whittier and Toni Barnes.

Frustrated, Susannah went in search of the head nurse. She was in one of the cubicles, checking to make sure everything was in order for the next patient. When Susannah complained that she hadn't been able to find out anything, Greta Schwinn shrugged and said, "Maybe it's just as well if she's that bad."

"But I hate not knowing. And have they found out what killed Julie Whittier?"

Nurse Schwinn's face closed and her lips met, clearly intending to keep something from slipping out. Then she must have changed her mind, because the lips opened again and she said, "All I know is, Matthews left that picnic this afternoon as if his shoes were on fire. *He'd* heard something, that's for sure. And judging from the expression on his face, he wasn't happy about what he'd heard."

"There must be rumors," Susannah pressed. "I know what this place is like. When you got here tonight, didn't anybody say anything? Some hint of what's wrong with Toni Barnes and Callie, and whether or not it's the same thing that Julie had. Didn't anybody even say whether or not it's contagious?"

The nurse avoided Susannah's eyes, busying herself with the folding of white hospital towels. "Oh, it's not catching," she said knowingly. "You can quit worrying about that right now."

"Then you *do* know something!"

The head nurse lifted her head, glancing around to make sure they were alone. Patsy and Bobs were busy elsewhere, the doctors were all in cubicles stitching or examining or treating, and

Will was out on an ambulance run. "Don't say a word," she cautioned Susannah. "Don't you say one word, because it's only rumor and rumors around here aren't worth two cents. It could be something entirely different by tomorrow morning, so if you repeat what I tell you, you might just look like a total fool when it turns out not to be true."

"*Tell* me!"

"I heard poison," Head Nurse Schwinn said very quietly. "Doesn't mean it's true. But that's what I heard. Poison."

chapter
23

Although Abby had already told Susannah of Dr. Maclaine's suspicions about Bradley Duval, she was shocked to hear the word "poison" in connection with the other cases. Did that mean that Abby, and everyone else who suspected Mrs. Duval, had been wrong about her? She could hardly be poisoning half the town.

All that week, the word "poison" rang in Susannah's mind. If finals hadn't helped keep her mind occupied, she would have gone crazy thinking about what Greta had told her. Poison? From what? From where? How did they *know* it was poison?

She didn't tell anyone, not even Abby, what Greta had said. But her silence was useless, because the rumor developed a life of its own. It spread throughout Med Center, and then into the surrounding city.

Reactions varied. Some said it was the water supply, contaminated by the lawn-chemical trucks spraying throughout the city. Others said it was the air, and people took to wearing white masks over their faces while doing yard work. Then there were those who were certain that the food supply delivered to local restaurants had spoiled in transit and the owners, afraid of financial disaster, had cooked and served the food, anyway, hoping no one would trace the source.

There were others, of course, who took the word "poison" more literally and decided there was a maniac loose in the city, armed with a deadly substance.

What confused everyone was that the victims had nothing in common. Will Jackson wasn't connected to Julie Whittier. He didn't live in the same neighborhood or eat at the same restaurants or have the same friends. Toni Barnes didn't know Julie Whittier *or* Will. Callie knew Will, but certainly hadn't eaten in any restaurants with him lately. The migraine victims who had fallen ill were two women, living in two entirely different areas of Grant, and three men whose wives and children had *not* fallen ill.

Nevertheless, when all of the rumors had been weighed and sifted and analyzed, most of the city focused on the water as the source of the "poison." Kettles and pots and pans of boiling water bubbled and gurgled on stoves all across the city. Sales of soda and bottled water skyrocketed.

To the surprise of certain staff members at Med Center, no sign of medical malpractice was revealed by Julie Whittier's autopsy. Those who weren't surprised were simply relieved, especially when Dr. Joe Sumner finally agreed to retire from surgery. Apparently, the threat of a possible malpractice suit had done what no one person had been able to do.

But they still didn't know what had killed Julie. Susannah and Abby heard that "renal failure" had been listed as the official cause of death. Julie's kidneys had shut down. No one seemed to know why though. "Anorexia" the rumor mill whispered, but Julie's mother and friends continued to angrily deny that diagnosis.

Julie was buried on a gray, misty Wednesday, the cemetery shrouded in thick fog. It was eerie, depressing. Abby had talked Susannah into going with her, and feeling sad and anxious, they left after the services.

Toni Barnes got no worse, but no better, either. Callie's condition continued to deteriorate. When Susannah called the hospital, Astrid told her that Caleb Matthews was beside himself with worry, and that Callie's mother, who didn't often leave the house because of her own illness, was spending day and night at her daughter's bedside.

There were six more cases of stomach distress during the first four days of that week. Only two of them were serious enough to warrant admission, and they were discharged after twenty-four hours with a diagnosis of gastroenteritis.

Bradley Duval recovered well enough to be discharged. However, his toxicology scan showed that he had been given a much larger dose of aspirin than his mother had related. Under insistent questioning by Dr. Maclaine, Beth Duval had broken down and admitted that she had lied. "I'd run out of his liquid aspirin," she had said tearfully, "and he was in so much pain, I thought my capsules, the ones they sent me home with the last time I came in with migraine, might help. They only gave me six." Her lips pursed in annoyance. "They never give you the whole bottle, you know, only a handful, doling them out as if they were rare jewels or something, when they're only one step above plain aspirin. Anyway, I hadn't used any of them yet, so I broke the capsules open and put the powder in his oatmeal. I thought they would give him more relief than children's, anyway, and I didn't see how they could hurt him. I was only thinking of him!"

An angry Dr. Maclaine had called in a social worker, and when the Duvals came to take their pale, shaky son home, they did not leave the hospital alone. The social worker went with them, prepared to interview both parents *and* the child and determine whether or not he really was simply accident-prone.

"Whatever else happens," Abby told Susannah and Kate when they heard that bit of news, "at least that little boy is getting some help."

"And if it hadn't been for him, and his swollen feet," Susannah pointed out, "Dr. Maclaine wouldn't have thought of poison."

"I heard," Kate said quietly, "that she's pushing for a forensic pathologist. That she said even the adult painkillers wouldn't have caused the symptoms she saw in that little boy. And my mother told me that sometimes, when the cause of death is in question, tissue samples are saved. They did that with Julie Whittier. Now Dr. Maclaine is insisting that someone who specializes in forensics be called in from Boston to study them. The hospital . . . meaning Caleb Matthews, of course . . . is resisting. He's afraid reporters will find out. He doesn't want the world to know that no one here can figure out why Julie died. My guess is, if Callie gets worse, and Caleb thinks those tissue samples might save her, he'll agree."

Abby and Kate had finished their finals on Thursday, Susannah on Friday, and now, on Saturday, they were back on duty. Although Abby was working at Rehab, she had joined Susannah and Kate in Grant Memorial's basement cafeteria for lunch.

Greta Schwinn, sitting at the table next to them with Patsy and Bobs, overheard their remarks and spoke up. "Well, I, for one, think that if it is poison, it's accidental. Maybe pesticides from those trucks all over town. I've been reading a lot of stuff lately about how careless we are with chemicals. They're all deadly, you know. You'd think a green lawn was more important than people's lives."

"Oh, that's not it!" Patsy disagreed. "For one thing, all of the victims didn't live in the same neighborhood. Some of them live in neighborhoods that don't approve of chemicals around their kids, and some were from other areas of town that could never afford lawn services. So it can't be the spraying. Anyway, if there was something in the water supply, the whole town would be sick. It's got to be something else."

Patsy's thick, blond hair hung loose around her shoulders. Susannah couldn't help thinking how different the nurse would look if she styled her hair like Dr. Barlow's Sunday afternoon date. But then she wouldn't be the same Patsy, casual and fun. Of course, she might still have Dr. Barlow in her life. It didn't seem to be bothering her that she didn't. Rumor had it that she was dating an intern, eight years her junior.

"Hold on, folks," Bobs warned, waving a carrot stick in the air. "May I just remind you that poison has *not* been found in any of the cases? Repeat, *not*. So far, this whole poison business is nothing but rumor and conjecture. But," she admitted, "it *is* hard to believe that no one in this stellar medical establishment has come up with an answer yet. In case you haven't noticed, the newspapers are having a field day with the rumors. They haven't exactly slandered Med Center yet, but they've come pretty damn close."

Greta Schwinn nodded. "I think Matthews is almost as upset about those articles as he is about his daughter. God, the man hates bad publicity! He's so afraid rumors will put a dent in hospital revenues. Which, of course, they might." She took a sip of her coffee. "The thing is, even if they identify something nasty in Whittier's tissues, they're not going to know where it came from. Or how it got there. Not right away, anyway. We could still have more victims."

Susannah was focusing on Patsy's comments. Eastridge, where Will lived, would be one of those neighborhoods that couldn't afford expensive lawn services. No poison there. But then, Will hadn't been that sick. Maybe he'd simply breathed in some of the pesticide fumes in another neighborhood when he was on an ambulance run. Just enough to make him very ill for a little while.

Since neither the nurses nor the volunteers had a clue about what the victims might have in common, they dropped the subject and talked instead about how much fun the picnic had been.

"If I ever decide to have a big party," Patsy said, "I'm hiring Tish Simone." Patsy's blue eyes sparkled. "Like for an engagement party, for instance. She really does a super job. Did you *see* those flowers? She grows them herself. Me, I'm death to anything green, no matter how much I spray and water and talk to them lovingly."

Susannah promised herself she would remember to pass on the compliment. Tish could use a boost in self-esteem.

"Engagement party? Is there something we should know, my friend the cradle robber?" Bobs teased with a grin. "Has your teenybopper intern friend popped the question?"

Patsy grinned, too. "Mike is twenty-four, Roberta dear. He's hardly a teenybopper. And no, he hasn't proposed. But I know he's thinking about it. I can see it in his eyes."

Bobs picked up her tray and rose to her feet. "That's what you said about Tom Barlow."

Patsy's face turned scarlet. "Well, you thought it, too. You convinced yourself he was going to ask you to marry him, even after you'd watched him dump the rest of us. I saw those bridal books in your locker. I could have told you that even if you did get him, it wouldn't last. But you never asked me. And I was right, wasn't I?"

"Ladies, please," Greta warned. "We *all* should have known better."

Unflustered, Bobs stood behind her chair, resting her tray on its back and said calmly, "You're right, I was an idiot. But I don't blame Tom for my foolishness. Or for yours, or Greta's.

We're the ones who didn't see the writing on the wall. Or, rather, *saw* it and ignored it." Her warm, brown eyes lifted to the ceiling, surveyed it, then moved to the walls until her gaze had encompassed most of the room. "It's this place. This place is all Tom Barlow cares about, all he'll *ever* care about."

The volunteers were staring at her. They had never heard Bobs talk so much before. Besides, her topic happened to be soured romances, something they could all relate to. "No woman is ever going to steal Tom Barlow's heart away from Med Center, I don't care how beautiful or sophisticated or brilliant she is. Don't you all *get* it? It wasn't that he was rejecting *me*. Or you, either, Patsy, or you, Greta. He was just choosing Med Center over us, that's all. Over *everyone*. So," another shrug, "why should I take it personally?"

Still, Susannah couldn't help feeling sorry for her. It must have been painful to get her hopes up and then have them dashed like that.

"You can have the bridal books," Bobs said, smiling at Patsy. "They're still in my locker, and it doesn't look like I'm going to be needing them."

"Sure you will." All forgiveness and smiles, Patsy said generously, "I'll give them back to you when I've gone through them. Sooner or later, your prince will come along, too."

"Well, he won't be twenty-four, I can tell you

that!" the taller nurse said dryly as all three nurses made their way out of the cafeteria. "I'd feel like his *mother*!"

"Oh, trust me," Patsy commented, laughing, "the last thing I feel like is Mike's mother!"

When they had gone, Abby said, "At least one of them has moved on after Jeremy's father. That intern, Mike, is adorable. Patsy's lucky."

"And," Kate added, "I heard Greta's going out Saturday night with Dr. Lobell. They'd make a great couple, I think. They're both short and round."

Susannah laughed as she stood up. "I never heard that was a requirement for romance, Kate . . . that both people have to be the same size and shape."

Kate stood up, too, nodding solemnly. "It's true. The law of romantic physics. I read it somewhere. Anyway, you don't have to worry, Susannah. You and Will are both tall and thin."

"So are you and Damon."

Abby let out a mock wail. "That better not be true, Kate! You'd better be making that up. Because Sid is tall and built like a fullback, and I'm short and . . . "

"Thankfully, *not* built like a fullback," Kate said, laughing.

chapter
24

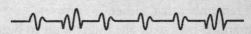

Helene Maclaine finally got her way. On Friday, word swept through the hospital that Caleb Matthews, frantic about his daughter's worsening condition, had agreed to call in a forensic pathologist to study Julie Whittier's tissue samples. The scientist was scheduled to arrive late that day.

While they waited, doctors approached Toni Barnes, who was responding well to treatment. She was still in ICU, and was very pale and lethargic. She was taking some nourishment though, and showed no signs of kidney or liver distress. A pair of white-coated doctors asked Toni to relate to them everything she had eaten or drunk during the week before being stricken.

Unfortunately, she could remember very little.

Susannah had gone upstairs to inquire about Callie, and was standing near the nurses' station, only a few feet from Toni's room, when she heard, "Miss Barnes, do you remember taking any medication, any drugs or stimulants on that Saturday?"

Toni answered uncertainly, "I don't think so. What *kind* of medication?"

"*Any* kind. Let me put it this way: Do you remember swallowing anything that wouldn't be classified as food or drink?"

"No. I don't even remember that day very well. The nurses tell me I took a bad fall, but I don't remember that, either."

Susannah hesitated. She didn't want to butt in where she didn't belong. But they were asking Toni a question that Toni couldn't answer. But *I* could, Susannah thought. At least I think I could.

There wasn't a nurse around to ask for advice. There seemed to be only one thing to do, and Susannah did it.

She walked to the door of the room and thrust her head in. "Excuse me. I think I can help."

The heads of two doctors, stethoscopes around their necks, swiveled to see who had spoken. "Ah, Susannah," said the man with graying hair and glasses. "You can help? How?" His colleague, a woman the same age, looked annoyed at the interruption.

Susannah entered the room. "Hi, Toni. You look better." Then she turned to the doctors. "I was in the drugstore that Saturday. Toni was there with, I guess, her mother. I didn't see them, but I overheard them talking."

Toni looked interested. "You did? I didn't see you."

"You were talking about an earache. In fact,

you were in the store to buy eardrops. You'd already been to the E.R., although I didn't see you there, and someone had treated you for the earache. They gave you some medication. Pain pills, I guess. You didn't want to take them, do you remember that?"

"No. But I do get earaches sometimes, when I've been swimming."

Susannah turned to the doctors. "I'm surprised Toni's mother didn't tell you about the pills. She knows Toni took them that day."

"Wait, I remember now. I told her I wasn't going to take them. But by early afternoon, I was in agony. My ear hurt *so* bad, like someone was sticking long, red-hot needles in there. So I took a couple of those capsules they gave me in the E.R. But I didn't tell my mom I'd changed my mind. I figured if she knew I was in that much pain, she'd make me stay home from Jeremy's party."

One of the doctors seemed disappointed. "You're talking about simple pain relief capsules. We get them from Grant Pharmaceuticals, stock them here by the bushelful."

The second doctor added, "We were thinking more along the lines of stimulants, something that might affect the kidneys and liver. Pain capsules wouldn't do that. You're positive you didn't take anything else?"

"I don't *do* drugs," Toni said indignantly, "if

193

that's what you're hinting. Anyway," she added smugly, "the nurse told me anything like that would have showed up in the blood tests. She said you were looking for that kind of thing. And then she said you didn't find it, which I knew you wouldn't. So why are you even asking?"

A white-jacketed shrug. "We may seem like old fogies to you, but we pay attention to what's going on outside of this medical complex. We know there are new, dangerous substances out there, and that you young people don't always realize *how* dangerous. It occurred to us that you may have ingested something we couldn't identify only because we hadn't seen it before."

"But," the other doctor added hastily, "we believe you. Thank you for the information, and it's good to see that you're feeling better."

When they had gone, Toni sank back against the pillow. "I thought the doctors here were so smart. My parents are always saying they are. So how come they can't find out what made me sick?"

"They will. It's just not that easy, I guess. Some forensic scientist is coming this afternoon to do some sleuthing. An expert. He'll figure it out. Whatever it is that put you in here, keep your fingers crossed that when they *do* know what it is, there'll be something they can give you to counteract the effects. Then you'll be out of here in no time." Susannah saw Connie Brewer approaching from the hallway. "I've gotta go now, Toni. I'm not even supposed to be in here. You take care. Maybe I'll check on you later, if I can."

Editorials and articles in the local newspapers had become more accusatory. Grant residents bombarded the hospital with telephone calls demanding answers.

No one had any.

Late that afternoon the forensic pathologist, a tiny, middle-aged woman with a streak of white in her short, straight, black hair, arrived at Med Center. No one in the E.R. saw her, but they did hear about her.

"Let's just hope she knows what she's doing," Bobs said grimly, in the process of admitting yet another gastrointestinal distress victim. The patient, an elderly woman who was a frequent patient at Grant because of chronic arthritis, was in so much pain, she could barely stand. An orderly had dashed off for a wheelchair. "Even my own mother is saying we should have found the cause of this stuff by now." She uttered a brief, harsh laugh. "At least she's not nagging me about getting married and giving her grandchildren right now."

The weekend, rainy and chilly, was spent reading and relaxing. No one called Susannah from

Emsee to say the cause of so much illness had been uncovered. But Abby did say she'd gone to Rehab on Sunday afternoon to see Sid, and there had been few cars in the E.R. parking garage. "I think people are afraid," she said. "They think they'll get sick if they go there."

There was no news on Monday, or on Tuesday. The E.R. remained oddly empty. If people were ill, they were taking their problems to their family doctor, or to the two smaller, private hospitals in the city.

The answer came on Wednesday evening, just as Susannah was getting ready to leave. She was meeting Abby, Sid, Kate, Damon, and Will on the steps outside. They were all going out for pizza to celebrate the end of the school year.

She had removed her smock, run a brush through her hair, and dabbed on lip gloss when Patsy, Greta, and Bobs moved silently into the room. When they were inside, standing in the center of the small, cluttered lounge, they remained silent, as if Susannah weren't there. Their faces looked blank, as if because they didn't know what to think, they weren't thinking anything.

Something had happened. Susannah's stomach turned over. Had someone else died? Toni Barnes? She'd seemed so much better. "What's wrong?" When no one answered, when they simply lifted their heads to stare at her blankly, she pressed, *"What? What's the matter?"*

It was Bobs who spoke, finally. "They know what it is."

"What *what* is?"

"What's making everyone sick."

"That doctor," Patsy added, "the one with the weird skunk's stripe in her hair, she found it."

"Well, what *is* it? *Tell* me!"

"Arsenic."

Susannah stared at all three of them. *Arsenic?* Arsenic killed Julie Whittier and made all of those other people, including Will, sick? Arsenic? "I didn't even know that stuff was around anymore. Isn't that something from the dark ages?"

"There's more," Bobs told her. "It gets worse." She paused dramatically, then added, "They don't know yet where those people got the poison. But they've narrowed it down to one of two places."

There was something in her blue eyes that made Susannah reluctant to ask the obvious question. But she had to know. "And those two places are?" Her voice was almost a whisper.

Bobs clasped her hands behind her back. There was no expression whatsoever in her face as she answered flatly and emphatically, "The first possibility is Grant Pharmaceuticals, because that's where Emsee's bottles of analgesic came from. But the second is right here in the E.R. If the bottles weren't tampered with at GP, then the tampering was done here, probably only to bottles that were already open."

"Here?" Susannah echoed.

Bobs nodded. "It seems there's a strong possibility that we've been dispensing poison to our patients in the E.R."

chapter
25

No sweat. I mean, they had to figure it out sooner or later. Okay by me. There've been enough victims to cause a real scandal. Enough of a scandal to bring this place down, and him with it.

Disgraceful . . . such an important medical complex, world-famous, passing out poison to innocent, unsuspecting victims.

But that's only one strike. One strike wouldn't be enough to ruin them. They could blame that much on tampering, and rant and rave about how their security system let them down and it wasn't their fault, blah, blah, blah.

So, on to strike two. They're not panicking because they're thinking, no problem, we have a drug on hand that will make our more seriously ill poison victims fit as fiddles in no time. We'll just trot on our rubber-soled feet to the drug cabinet and help ourselves. Then our spokesperson can go to the papers and say, "See? We solved the problem, we cured our patients just like we're supposed to do. All is well in the world of medicine."

Ha. Guess again, folks.

I'm not stupid. I'd have to be pretty dumb to take all that time and trouble and then leave the antidote lying around to solve their problem quickly and quietly. That might have allowed the whole thing to blow over in no time, with no permanent repercussions.

No way. We didn't have that much on hand to begin with. I got rid of every last trace of the stuff. Surprise, surprise!

That makes two strikes against them. First, the tampering, which they never should have allowed to happen. And second, finding the cupboard bare. Inexcusable. They're going to have to send out for what they need. That takes time. Such inefficiency. Such sloppy inventorying. What a way to run a hospital. The press will know about it. I'll see to that.

And the looks on their faces when they heard the word "arsenic"! It was worth every scary moment of sneaking the bottles out, one at a time. I only took the ones that had already been opened . . . a different one from each cubicle . . . so I wouldn't have to worry about replacing the seal. Taking the capsules apart was a piece of cake. GP has never had a tampering scandal, so they never worried about whether or not the capsules themselves were tamperproof.

They weren't.

Right now, all anyone is concerned about is the cure. Later, when they start pointing fingers, they'll point to Grant Pharmaceuticals, because the med-

ication came from there. Every lab technician in the place will be a suspect. I hope Tish Simone is one of them. He still has her on his mind, I know he does. If she hadn't pressed him about marriage and kids before he was ready, he'd still be with her.

Everyone knows she uses pesticides to grow those stupid flowers of hers. And not a single person suspects that some of those little white bottles of painkiller took a side trip to my house.

But eventually, they'll realize that it wasn't her. I want them to. They have to know the truth. I want them to know. Because I am the third strike. I will be the straw that broke the camel's back, the final nail in Med Center's coffin, the icing on the cake. The guilty party . . . yours truly . . . is someone they trusted implicitly, someone they allowed to have access to every inch of their facility, someone who was an integral part of Med Center. Perfect. How careless of them, how foolish! Unforgivable. How could any patient ever feel comfortable in that facility again?

I have to be that third strike. Let them suspect whoever they want at first, but when push comes to shove, I have to let the world know I did it.

I don't care what happens to me, anyway. As long as I take them down with me. That's the most important thing. That's the whole thing.

If they're too stupid to figure it out, I'll tell them myself. I wish he could be there. I'd love to see the look on his face. He'll never believe it. Of course,

I'm not stupid enough to expect him to care what happens to me. All he'll really care about is that his beloved Med Center is in deep, deep doo-doo. And since I know that, I can't be the tiniest bit sorry about what I did.

No remorse, that's what they'll say in the newspapers.

And they'll be right.

No remorse at all.

chapter
26

Susannah had been in shock ever since she'd learned the truth about the poison. She had tried so hard to take in the news the nurses had delivered, but it wasn't computing. Will said, that night as a huge pizza lay untouched on the table in front of Susannah and her friends, that Emsee's rumored involvement made sense.

"Easy access," he had pointed out. "Those bottles are in every cubicle at Emsee. They're not locked in the drug cabinet like the heavier stuff. Anyone could have got at them."

Sid and Kate agreed. But Abby leaned more toward Grant Pharmaceuticals as the culprit. "All they know so far is that the arsenic was in the analgesic capsules. But those pills *come* from GP. So I don't see why everyone is blaming Emsee. That poison could have been put into those bottles at GP, before they ever *got* to Med Center."

To Susannah's horror, she immediately thought of Tish. Tish worked at GP. She had access to those bottles. Which would mean nothing, except that she was probably pissed at Emsee because Dr. Barlow had, according to Bobs, chosen Emsee over Tish. Which should also mean nothing, because people didn't run around punishing a *place*, did they?

But they *did*. People sometimes wreaked vengeance in post offices and government buildings and courthouses.

No one had brought a gun into or bombed Med Center. But ruining its reputation was probably a better way to get even.

Then there was the pesticide. Will had announced that the pathologist thought the arsenic had most likely been purchased in pesticide form. And Tish grew beautiful flowers. Could you do that without using pesticides? Their own gardener, Paolo, used them. So did the Barlows' gardener, and Patsy had mentioned "spraying."

"How can they be so sure *where* the poison came from?" Susannah had to ask.

Kate took a sip of milk, leaving a white mustache on her upper lip. She wiped it off with a paper napkin. "Computer. First they looked up the E.R. records to see which of the patients had left there with medication. Then they cross-checked to see which ones had left with the *same* medication. All of the patients who'd fallen ill *after* their visit to E.R. had taken home at least a few capsules of the same painkiller. Not every patient treated in the E.R. *did* come back sicker

than when they ___
sules left were asked to bring ___ who had cap-
see so the doctor could analyze them. Some had
poison in them, some didn't. Some had a lot,
some had only a tiny bit. But those capsules are
definitely the source."

"So the only question now," Will said, "is,
were the bottles tampered with at Emsee, after
they'd already been opened and were just sitting
on the counters in the cubicles? Or did it happen
before they ever left GP?"

Susannah hated both possibilities. "Why were
you sick?" she asked Will. "You didn't take any of
the capsules home. You told Izbecki you didn't
need them."

"I didn't need them, because I already *had*
some at home. Got them from the E.R. when I
sprained my ankle at track practice. I had taken
two the morning of the race, for my headache."

"You didn't tell us that when you came in after
you collapsed."

Will shrugged. "I didn't think it was important. We were focusing on what I ate, so I forgot
about the pills."

Susannah realized that had been true of Julie
Whittier, as well. She had probably been taking
the painkiller ever since she left the hospital, the
poison accumulating in her system until the
amount became lethal. Toni had taken them for

... well, Caleb Matthews an ear... ication home from Emsee for his ailing wife fairly often. The pills were probably in their house somewhere. Then there were the migraine patients, and many other patients who had been given the medication in E.R. for aches and pains and scrapes. If every bottle and every capsule had been laced with a high dosage of the poison, the halls of Emsee would be strewn with corpses.

Susannah shuddered.

"It could be worse," Kate offered, holding her slice of pizza in front of her as if she were studying it. "Mom says Med Center has a drug that will help. Can't remember its name . . . sounds like a coin, I think . . . dime . . . dimer-something. It's used to treat arsenic poisoning, but only if there isn't already kidney or liver damage. Callie and Toni are okay that way so far. If they get the drug right away, it might do the trick. Most of the other victims will be okay without it, but Callie and Toni have to have it . . . especially Callie."

While the news of an available treatment was reassuring, it didn't change the depressing fact that both Med Center and Grant Pharmaceuticals were under suspicion.

Still, when Susannah and Abby arrived in the E.R. on Thursday morning, they expected at least a slight lifting of the morbid atmosphere that had plagued the hospital since the word "poison" had become fact, not rumor. At least now they knew what was causing so much sickness. That should help a little.

Instead, they walked into a shouting match between Dr. Lobell and a cowering Patsy Keene.

"What do you mean, we don't *have* any? That's impossible!"

She spread her hands helplessly. "They haven't been able to find it. We did have it, but it's gone. All of it. It's just gone. It's still listed on the inventory sheet, but it's not in the cabinet."

"That's ridiculous!" Dr. Lobell's face, nice-looking when he was calm, was ugly with fury. "This is not a rare drug we're talking about here! You must have misunderstood. I'll call myself and find out where the hell they put it."

And so he did. Susannah and Abby, and every other nurse and doctor and orderly in the E.R., all idled by a telling lack of patients, stood by, openly listening.

When the physician turned away from the telephone, it was clear that he'd received the same answer that Patsy Keene had given him. There was no dimercaprol, the drug needed to help seriously ill patients like Callie and Toni, anywhere in the hospital. And none of the other hospitals in the complex stocked it. If one of their patients needed the drug, they would simply send them to Grant Memorial for treatment.

Susannah was surprised and dismayed when,

in answer to Patsy's suggestion that they call Grant Pharmaceuticals, right next door, for a fresh supply of the drug, Dr. Lobell answered sarcastically, "Now *there's* a smashing idea! Why not get our antidote from a company that, for all anyone knows, sent us the poison in the *first* place? Never mind that any cure that comes from GP could be as contaminated as the medication that made these people sick!"

Patsy's face flushed scarlet.

Susannah was sickened. The newspapers had printed stories implicating her father's drug company. But the investigation had barely begun. Lobell had no right to say such things.

"Your suggestion happens to be useless, anyway," Dr. Lobell hurled at Patsy. "Grant Pharmaceuticals has been closed down until further investigation. Haven't you heard? They are *not* open for business which, if you ask me, is a brilliant idea."

Susannah gasped. GP had been shut down? She hadn't been told. Her father hadn't been at breakfast, and her mother either hadn't known or didn't want to mention it.

Kate moved from the nurses' desk to stand beside Susannah. "He has to blame GP," she told Susannah quietly. "All the doctors do. Because if GP isn't to blame, then Emsee is, and they can't handle that idea."

Susannah nodded, but she was wondering who the citizens of Grant were blaming. The pharmaceutical company that sold the medicine to the hospital? Or the hospital that dispensed it to its patients?

chapter
27

Friday morning dawned as chilly and foggy as the day of Julie Whittier's funeral. Visibility on Linden Hill was close to zero when Susannah went to the window. The eerie gray mist made her shiver with dread. This was the morning the LifeFlite helicopter was off to Boston to pick up a supply of dimercaprol, the drug needed to off-set the arsenic poisoning in the more serious cases at Med Center. If the weather prohibited the trip, Caleb Matthews would go ballistic.

"Can't they use some other drug?" Susannah had asked Patsy when Dr. Lobell stormed off to consult with the hospital's administration. "I mean, now that they know what the poison is, isn't there any other medication that will work?"

"Lobell wants dimercaprol, he'll get dimer-caprol," the nurse answered grimly.

When it became definite that the drug was not to be found anywhere at Med Center, Matthews had located the nearest supply of it. He was sending LifeFlite, the hospital's heli-copter service, off to Boston to bring back the drug. Because Dr. Lobell was unwilling to leave his patients, Dr. Barlow, who had friends at the Boston hospital, had volunteered to take his place, and he had invited Jeremy along. Once he recovered from his astonishment, Jeremy was thrilled. Not only would he be spending some private time with his father, he'd get to ride in a helicopter. The forensic pathologist, her work finished, would be returning home on the same flight.

Standing at her bedroom window watching the thick fog swirl around the trees and bushes below, Susannah wondered if the helicopter would even be able to take off.

She dressed hurriedly in jeans and a warm sweater she'd already put away for the season, thinking she wouldn't need it again. It was too chilly for a T-shirt this morning.

All Abby said when Susannah picked her up for the trip to Med Center was, "Think they'll take off?"

"I don't know. Callie was worse last night when I left. Her father might insist on a takeoff, even if someone else says not to."

There was an air of depression in the E.R. Everyone knew the hospital was in serious trouble, and no one knew how to deal with it. The obvious theft of the dimercaprol listed on the drug inventory sheet seemed to some like clear proof that a hospital employee was guilty of the poisoning from start to finish. Others wanted to believe that it would be just as easy for an employee from Grant Pharmaceuticals, which was located nearby, to slip into Grant Memorial, steal several of the bottles, take them somewhere else to do their tampering, and then return them in a second visit, stealing the dimercaprol during one of those two visits.

That theory made no sense to Susannah. The analgesic capsules would have been accessible. But the dimercaprol would not have been. Only someone who worked in the hospital would know where to locate that drug. To her, though she hated to admit it, that meant only someone she knew well from her hours of volunteering could be the guilty party.

"It could have been an outsider," Sid had volunteered, trying in vain to lift spirits. "Or a patient, while no one was watching."

No one believed that, not for a second. The guilty party had to know something about medicine. And the process of contamination, especially when it involved varying the amounts of poison placed in each capsule, would have been far too time-consuming for a patient who was being quickly treated and released.

Though GP had been shut down, the hospital had not. But they weren't busy. And although it continued to function efficiently, suspicion was running high. If the criminal was one of their own, who was it?

There were no smiles in the E.R., there was no light, casual conversation, no silly antics because of so much downtime. There was only a deep, heavy silence that made Susannah feel as if someone had painted all of the windows black.

The fog continued, as thick and heavy as the atmosphere inside the building. The same question was on everyone's lips: "Are they taking off?"

They didn't learn the answer until shortly after ten o'clock. The LifeFlite helicopter had left the pad on top of Grant Memorial at precisely nine-fifty, against the advice of all authorities.

"Matter of life and death," an orderly named Joey Rudd told Susannah. "That's how they got permission. Said it was a matter of life and death. And I guess it is."

Depression turned to anxiety as the day wore on and they awaited the return of the helicopter. Whatever happened to Med Center because of the poisonings, the only thing that mattered now was getting LifeFlite and its essential cargo back to Grant Memorial safely.

While they waited, the E.R. was virtually empty.

"Fog's worse," Will said as he and Susannah drank coffee in the basement cafeteria. They

213

were seated at a small table beside a window. "That copter shouldn't have taken off."

"Maybe you wouldn't feel that way if Callie was *your* daughter."

When Will was paged over the P.A. system, Susannah went with him. They knew the minute they stepped out of the stairwell into the E.R. lobby that something had happened. The anxiety level had risen, they could feel it in the air. "Uh-oh," Will said softly when he saw Astrid hurrying toward them. "Somethin's goin' down."

"What?" Susannah was the first to ask when the head nurse reached them.

"They have the dimercaprol," she said hurriedly. "They're here. But they can't land on the copter pad. The fog is too thick. They're looking for another spot, somewhere on the grounds. We're in touch by radio, and they've asked for an ambulance to stand by. Will?"

He was already on the run toward the back entrance.

"I want to go, too," Susannah said, turning to follow him.

"We're *all* going," Astrid said quietly. "We've no patients right now, and we may be needed out there."

Susannah stared at her. "You think they're going to crash, don't you?" She thought of Jeremy, on his first helicopter ride, and his father. "You think they can't possibly land safely in this fog."

Astrid turned away. "I never said that. All I meant was, Caleb Matthews is waiting with bated breath for that dimercaprol. If we're out there when the copter lands, one of us can race back here with it and make the man happy."

But Susannah knew she hadn't meant that. It wouldn't take the entire E.R. staff to bring back one small box of medication. Astrid hadn't meant that at all.

chapter
28

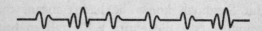

When the E.R. staff emerged into the chilly fog, Susannah found Abby and Sid taking shelter under the building's roof overhang.

"We heard they were coming in," Abby said. "Couldn't wait inside. Think they'll make it okay?"

Susannah didn't answer. "Will's out there somewhere in an ambulance. I don't know how they can see to drive in this. I can just barely make out the outline of Rehab, and it's not that far away."

"I see the ambulance," Sid announced, leaning forward in his chair. He pointed. "Over there, see it? Will just jumped out."

Susannah strained to see. "Isn't that Rehab's picnic area? There are picnic tables in the way!" Even as she spoke, the fog cleared slightly and she saw Will and two of his partners rushing out into the wide, flat, grassy area to hastily drag three wooden tables away.

Then the noise of the helicopter drowned out all other sound, and a moment later, Susannah saw it, a large, egg-shaped, blue-and-white air-

216

craft, barely visible through the thick, smoky gray overhead.

Patsy Keene yelled, "There it is!" and all eyes lifted. Other staff members and maintenance personnel had emerged from the building, the crowd swelling to more than two dozen mist-dampened, anxious spectators.

Susannah kept her eyes on the sky. "He keeps hovering, like he's not sure he wants to land here at all." She had to shout to make herself heard above the engine's noise.

"He probably can't see the ground, because of the fog," Sid shouted back. "He needs someone on the ground, directing him."

"We'll go," Bobs volunteered, grabbing Patsy Keene's red-sweatered elbow and dragging her away from the shelter of the building. "We'll wave something at him, signal him into the middle of the clearing."

"Will can do it," Susannah called after them, but the two white-uniformed women were already out in the open, running toward the picnic clearing. As they ran, Patsy stripped free her red cardigan and began waving it in the air.

At the same time, Will and one of his partners moved out into the clearing. One of them, Susannah couldn't tell which, was waving a huge flashlight.

"Looks like they're going to have plenty of help landing!" Sid shouted.

"They're going to need it," Astrid yelled back.

Will was standing almost directly beneath the copter, waving his arms, signalling to the pilot that it was okay to land. Patsy and Bobs arrived in the clearing, remaining on the opposite side of it. Patsy continued to wave the red sweater.

Finally, the helicopter began its descent.

Silence descended upon the group of onlookers. The only sound was the steady chuggity-chug of the helicopter as it started down.

And then Abby, her voice shaking, said, "The flagpole. What about the flagpole? Don't they *see* it?"

Due to the inclement weather, the flag itself was not flying. But the thick silver metal pole was there, standing tall and rigid on Bobs and Patsy's side of the clearing, reaching straight up toward the steadily descending machine.

When Abby spoke, all eyes focused on the flagpole.

Orderly Joey Rudd cupped his hands around his mouth and shouted, "Flagpole, flagpole!" to Will and the two nurses. But Susannah knew there was no way they could hear. They were too close to the aircraft.

"They'll wave him away from the pole," Sid yelled. "Then he'll have plenty of room."

Everyone waited silently for the helicopter to veer sideways. That didn't happen. It continued to descend in a straight path.

"They can't *see* the top of the flagpole from the ground," Susannah cried. "It's hidden in the fog. And they're focusing so hard on the helicopter, they're forgetting the pole is standing right there in front of them."

No one could be sure what was going to happen. The only thing they could be certain of was that the flagpole wasn't about to move.

"*Do* something!" Abby screamed.

The red sweater continued to wave. The flashlight continued to shine faintly through the thick fog. And the helicopter continued to descend in a straight path.

Susannah had just moved away from the protection of the building to get a better look when Will noticed the flagpole's base. She saw him shout to the nurses and his partners, saw him point frantically toward the silver column, saw him throw his arm out in a warning gesture then, when he must have felt he wasn't being understood by anyone, break into a run toward the flagpole to point it out.

Susannah took another few steps forward.

The helicopter made it below the top of the flagpole without incident, and with room to spare.

Abby let out a heartfelt sigh of relief.

Too soon.

She had forgotten about the helicopter's swirling blades. She had barely exhaled when the tip of one grazed the metal pole with what seemed to be a glancing blow. "Hardly a tap," Sid would say later in wonderment. "Hardly touched it."

But what looked from the ground, in poor visibility, to be no more than a tap, was enough to knock the blue-and-white machine dangerously off balance. They all saw the aircraft shudder with the blow. Then the steady downward descent became a tipping, tilting, out-of-control swaying, as if the helicopter might be having a convulsion.

Tearing her eyes away from the machine, Susannah lowered them to Will. His three partners had already begun backing away, their eyes on the troubled aircraft, but Will was standing almost directly beneath it. Its descent had become a bizarre, convulsive journey, and there was Will, still standing in a spot that was clearly now in harm's way.

"Will?" she called above the roar, which, she realized as she shouted, was beginning to turn into an unhealthy coughing and chugging and choking. "Will! Get away, move, get *out* of there! Something's wrong!" Unable to make him hear her, Susannah broke into a run, straight toward Will.

Later, she would say in a dazed voice, "It fell out of the sky. It just fell right out of the sky."

When it fell, it came straight down, and although Susannah thought she heard screaming from inside the machine, she knew that was impossible over the horrible, discordant sound the helicopter made as it came swiftly down.

She found only enough voice to scream Will's name one more time.

Then the aircraft hit the ground with a thunderous grinding sound that Susannah knew she would never forget. Bits and pieces of metal flew in all directions, blades crumpled like tinfoil, glass exploded, sending shards and chunks out into the fog as if they were on a search mission.

Something slammed into her left arm, something sharp, causing a sudden, stinging pain. Before she had time to look down and see what had hit her, another object pierced her right shoulder, sending a spray of red shooting out from beneath her sweater.

People were already running out of the different hospitals, some with stretchers in hand.

When the grinding, shattering noises ceased, Susannah, reaching toward the wound in her shoulder to stop the flow of blood, looked for Will with eyes dulled by shock.

She didn't see him anywhere.

chapter
29

Stretchers rushed back and forth between the crash site and Grant Memorial. An ambulance would have been a waste of time, when legs could run and arms could lift unconscious victims and race across the short distance and into the E.R.

In the E.R., Astrid said to a semiconscious Susannah, "Just lie still. Don't move. We have to stop the flow of blood."

"Will?"

"Never mind Will. He's fine. You lie still." As she worked, she muttered, "Never seen anything like that in my *life*! Nothin' but a hunk of twisted metal out there, just a bunch of blue-and-white itty-bitty pieces!"

"Dr. Barlow? Jeremy?"

"They're okay, I'm tellin' you. You listen, girl, if you don't lie quiet, I'm gonna have to shoot you full of dope. Dr. Barlow's got a broken arm that'll keep him on the sidelines for a while. Relax and spend some time with his kid, maybe. Jeremy, he's got himself a concussion and a shat-

222

tered elbow, and he's havin' a fit 'cause Izbecki had to shave his head to stitch up a nasty cut on his skull. Worried about his hair not growin' back in the right way. Men, I swear they're ten times as vain as women ever were!"

The pilot, Susannah learned later, was not so lucky. The helicopter had landed on its nose before crumpling into an accordion-like mass, and he had taken the full brunt of the crash. He was dead before rescue workers managed to cut their way through to him.

It was Sid who found Will, Abby told her. Sid was the only one to notice, just seconds before the helicopter hit, that Will had had the presence of mind to dive out of the way. While Abby and Kate ran with Susannah's stretcher to the E.R., Sid speedily wheeled his chair over to a dim, foggy corner of the building closest to the crash site. "Will?" he called when he saw an enormous, muddy tennis shoe.

Will was conscious, suffering from lacerations and bruises, but no broken bones. His first inquiry of Sid, according to Abby, was, "Is Susannah okay?"

The most horrifying news given Susannah, only after she had been stitched up and mildly sedated, was that Patsy Keene was dead. She hadn't moved as fast as Bobs when the helicopter came down. Her coworkers in the E.R. were shocked and saddened, but were grateful that both nurses, considered heroes by all, hadn't died.

Finding the dimercaprol in the wreckage took a long time, sending an already overtaxed Caleb Matthews nearly over the edge. It was finally located, and dispatched with haste to the waiting patients.

Still, in spite of that bit of good news, the atmosphere in the E.R. was dismal. It wasn't just the accident, or the death of a popular nurse. There was, incredibly, more. While everyone was outside watching as the tragedy unfolded, Caleb Matthews had been informed by investigators that the E.R. at Grant Memorial was definitely responsible for the tampering and that Grant Pharmaceuticals was off the hook.

"Every patient had been treated in the E.R. before they fell ill. Every *one*. We don't know which individual is the guilty party, but the tampering absolutely took place here. Therefore, the investigation will be intensified here."

It didn't take long for that news to filter down to the E.R.

"Good news, bad news," Dr. Izbecki said as he put the finishing touches on Susannah's stitches. "The good news is, this won't break us. Even with the inevitable lawsuits, we're not folding, which I suspect is what someone had in mind. The bad news is, that *someone* is one of *us*, and we don't know who."

While Susannah was horrified that it was an Emsee employee, someone she *worked* with, she was too grateful to be alive, and to have Jeremy and Will and Jeremy's father alive, to think about the poisonings now. Besides, she hurt. A lot. She'd think about what it all meant later.

That opportunity came the following morning. She had been kept overnight for observation in a small room on the third floor. Shortly after nine, Will, Kate, and Abby walked into her room, their faces solemn. Will, his face a map of scratches and bruises and swellings, was carrying a folded newspaper.

"Bad news," he said, sitting down on Susannah's bed. He thrust the paper at her. "Here, better read it for yourself."

Susannah opened the paper and read the Letter to the Editor that Will had circled in red pen.

I want the city of Grant, I want the world, I want everyone to know that the person who poisoned all those people works for Med Center. This employee works in the E.R. and had access to the analgesic capsules. This employee took the bottles home, one at a time, took them apart, added arsenic, which was purchased in pesticide form in an old Grain and Feed warehouse sixty miles from Grant in a farming community. The town's name is Porterville. Anyone who wants to, can check this out. It's the truth. The owner might lie, because he's

225

not even supposed to have this stuff anymore, but if his warehouse is searched, other canisters will be uncovered.

This is the truth: First, Med Center made it possible for an employee to tamper with medication and dispense it to patients. Second, they were then unable to diagnose the cause of so many illnesses. They had to call in outside help. Third, they had no available antidote on hand.

All of these things are unforgivable. I ask the people of Grant, as a concerned citizen, to refuse to patronize an establishment that cares so little for their welfare. There are other medical facilities in town, good ones. If you care about your safety, you would do well to hold Med Center accountable for its actions.

> *Sincerely,*
> *A Concerned Citizen*

Susannah let the paper fall into her lap. She lifted her head to look at Will with sickened eyes. "Who wrote this?"

He shrugged. "No one knows. It could have been anyone with a grudge against the hospital. But the press is outside on the front steps, and they're out for blood."

"The good news," Abby said hastily, unhappy about the look on Susannah's face, "is, Toni's better this morning. And so is Callie."

"*That's* good news?" Kate asked dryly. But she was smiling.

"Is this going to ruin Med Center?" Susannah asked quietly. "Will people stop coming here?"

Will laughed. He reached out and took her hand in his. "Never happen! We'll probably have a few lawsuits. Can't blame people for that, right? But it'd take a lot more than that to bring Emsee down." More seriously, he added, "I do agree with Izbecki, though. His theory is that someone wanted to ruin us. Someone who had an axe to grind."

"Who?" Kate and Susannah asked at the same time.

Will shrugged again. "Beats me."

Patsy Keene's funeral was attended by every Med Center employee who could get away. The fog had lifted and the sun had taken its place. But the improved weather did nothing to lift anyone's spirits.

On the following Tuesday, when Susannah, her arm and shoulder still sore but healing nicely, arrived in the E.R., Kate was waiting for her, a gloomy expression on her face.

"I hate to ask," she said reluctantly, "but I need you to help me do something. My mom asked me, and I don't want to do it alone, okay?"

"What is it?"

Kate's mouth drooped. "Patsy's mom is coming to get her things today. Mom wants us to clean out her locker."

Susannah didn't want to. "Why can't one of the maintenance people do it? That's too gruesome, Kate. We *knew* her. I can't."

"You know my mom. She doesn't want strangers doing it. She wants someone who knew Patsy to do it. And Bobs can't, she's too upset. That leaves us, I guess."

There wasn't much in Patsy's locker. The bridal magazines Bobs had given her. An extra sweater, a white cardigan with a bloodstain on one cuff. Two romance novels, their pages well thumbed. Hairbrush. Comb. Mascara. "So," Kate asked as she piled the items into a cardboard box as Susannah handed them to her, "any idea who the guilty party is?" Toothbrush and toothpaste. A box of tissues. A picture of Patsy and Dr. Barlow, dressed for a formal occasion, Patsy in a red, strapless gown, Barlow in a tuxedo. Both were smiling.

"No." Susannah found it painful, handling items that only last week, someone had been using, and now never would again. Notebook. Pens. Half a dozen barrettes in different colors, which Patsy had used when things got really hectic in the E.R. and she needed to pin her blond, curly hair away from her face. An extra pair of pantyhose, and, on the floor of her locker, a pair of black suede high heels. "Must have kept them here in case Mike asked her out on the spur of the moment," Susannah said, placing the shoes in the box.

The letter was underneath the shoes. Had it been in an envelope, Susannah never would have read it. But it was just a sheet of paper, lying print side up on the floor of the locker.

She recognized it the minute she saw it. The same expression appeared in her eyes that had been there the first time she read it, when Will brought it to her printed in a newspaper.

She bent down slowly and picked it up. Read it again. Held it out to Kate to read. "Oh, my god," Kate breathed when she had finished. She lifted her head, her eyes meeting Susannah's. "She *hated* this place? Wanted it ruined? *Why?* Why would she hate Med Center?"

Susannah reached into the box and lifted out the picture of Patsy and Dr. Barlow. "Remember what Bobs said in the cafeteria that day? How Dr. Barlow would never choose a woman over Med Center? Maybe that's why."

Kate let that sink in. Then her eyes widened. "She knew he was in that helicopter," she said, the words dragging out of her reluctantly, revealing how much they pained her. "Susannah. Patsy wasn't waving that copter *away* from the flagpole. She *wanted* it to hit the pole!"

"No. No! That can't be true. It was just too foggy, Kate. She couldn't have seen the top of that flagpole from the ground."

"Maybe not." Kate's voice was bleak. "But she could see the *bottom* of it. She wanted the helicopter to crash with Dr. Barlow in it, and maybe she didn't want to get out of its way. Will did. Bobs did. The other paramedics did. Couldn't Patsy have, too, if she'd really wanted to? But she'd already mailed the letter to the newspaper, so she must have thought she'd ruined Emsee. Maybe she didn't care if she died."

epilogue

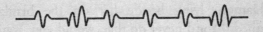

They no longer took their lunches to the picnic ground. They couldn't bear to be that close to the site of the helicopter crash. The remains were gone now, but the lawn was still scarred from ripping, gouging shards of metal. Instead, they gathered on a blanket in a park-like area behind Rehab.

"I saw Patsy take one of the bottles," Susannah admitted as she opened a can of soda. "I saw her put it in her uniform pocket. But I thought she was just taking it to another cubicle."

Abby was still in shock over all that had been revealed in the past few days. At Patsy's condo, the police had found a diary in which she explained in graphic detail exactly what she was doing, and why. "Well, *I* thought she was crazy about that intern, that Mike person. She acted like she was."

Will made a sound of disgust. "You're half right. She *was* crazy."

"Sick," Kate corrected. "She was sick. That happens to some people when they want something so badly and can't have it. It throws them off balance, just like that helicopter." She unwrapped a tuna sandwich. "I can't believe she let a broken heart screw up her life like that. And *end* it."

Damon, lying beside her on the blanket, grinned. "You'd never do that, would you, Katie? If you were gonna give arsenic to anyone, it'd be the guy who broke your heart, right?"

"Absolutely. And don't you forget it, Damon Lawrence!"

"I saw your friend Tish having dinner with Dr. Barlow last night," Abby told Susannah.

Jeremy, sitting with his back against a tree, appeared to swallow hard.

Susannah's jaw dropped. "You *did*? Are you sure it was her?"

"It was her. She looked gorgeous." Abby turned to look at Jeremy. "So, whadya think, Jeremy? I know you don't like Tish. Are you mad at your dad?"

Jeremy's face flushed, but he shook his head. "Not really. He could do worse, I guess." He laughed wryly. "I think what Patsy did because of him made him slow down a little. Quit playing the field. And I'm butting out. The thing is," he added ruefully, "I *liked* Patsy Keene. Shows you how much I know about women. So from now on, I'll let him pick his own dates."